LAVA CAKE AND LIES

MOONSTONE BAKERY
BOOK ONE

NOVA WALSH

1

It never fails that when you are most in need of sleep, you are least likely to get it. And that was certainly the case for me on my first morning in my new home of Moonstone Bay, California.

My cat, Shortcake, jumped squarely onto my stomach just as my phone started to buzz near my head. I opened one eye. There was light coming through the tattered curtains hanging in the small window nearby, but not much of it. Who could be calling at such an ungodly hour?

Of course, it was my mother.

"Ginny! I was worried!" She whined into my ear as soon as I answered. "You didn't call me last night!"

I rolled onto my side and Shorty rolled off my belly, then curled up next to me and started to purr. I stroked his back and tried to channel calm. "It was after midnight when we got in. I thought you'd rather I waited until morning."

"I was worried," she said again.

When wasn't my mother worried? If it was genuine worry, it wouldn't bother me so much, but more often than not, my mother's concerns centered more on how my actions would reflect on her. Case in point...

"I don't know why you're out there all by yourself. What are people going to think? It looks like you ran away. This whole thing feels so...impulsive, Virginia. It's not like you."

I rolled my eyes and sat up in the bed. Shorty moved to my lap and started purring again. Decades of being deliberate had led to a complete implosion of my life, so it seemed that a little impulsivity might be just what I needed. Which was exactly why I'd fled my hometown of San Francisco and moved into a crumbling bungalow in the sleepy coastal town of Moonstone Bay. I wanted to distance myself from that deliberate me and regroup. Maybe start over completely.

As I looked around the shabby room I'd woken up in, though, mother's protests worked their way deeper into my psyche. *What had I done?*

Cobwebs hung everywhere. The mattress I sat on was full of lumps and creaks. Dust was so thick that I saw cat prints along with my thick sock prints on the floor. I sneezed as I realized it, and Shorty did too. We had a *lot* of work to do.

My ex-husband Christopher and I had bought the beach bungalow on a whim a few years before. It was back when we were newlyweds and thought we were happy together. Our plan had been to fix the place up and use it as a rental property, but both of us were so busy at the time with our fledgling law careers that we hadn't had the energy to invest in the place. So it sat alone and neglected, collecting copious amounts of dust and spiders and who knew what else ever since.

I snapped back to it, realizing that my mother was still complaining in my ear.

"You went to Stanford Law, sweetheart. You can't just walk away from that."

Grabbing the sheet, I rubbed it over the phone. "What's that, mom? Sorry, you're breaking up!" A little more rubbing and then I pressed End Call.

If I never heard "Stanford Law" again, I would be thrilled. I didn't need any more reminders of what I was walking away from. Not this morning, at least.

I pulled the blanket tighter around myself, suddenly shivering. February on the Northern California coast was frigid, and we'd gotten in so late the night before I hadn't been able to figure out the space heater that hung on the wall so I'd piled on the blankets and sweaters and fallen asleep with Shorty for a little added warmth.

Shivering, I finally braved the cold, and threw off the covers to make a dash to the heater. But no matter how much I tried, the thing would not turn on.

After several minutes of fruitless fiddling, I couldn't get it to work. Exasperated and freezing, I hit it with my fist, but still no hot air came out. It must be broken. Gritting my teeth, I gave up on the thing and pulled my coat on, then headed into the main living space to give my new home a good look. Shorty trailed behind. I'd had the wherewithal to buy myself a cup of coffee before pulling in the night before and I popped it in the microwave, grateful that this at least was functioning.

As I waited for it to heat up, I watched Shorty stretch and strut through the place, leaving a trail of paw prints everywhere. Then he jumped up on the counter and gave me a very demanding meow.

I picked him up and put him on the ground, then grabbed a can of cat food and filled a bowl, then set it down for him. "What do you think, bud? Is this crazy or what?" He paid me no attention, but tucked into his breakfast.

I sighed. The furniture that had come with the house was

old and smelly. I would at the very least need to replace it and get this place cleaned properly. I thought about hiring a maid. That's what I would have done in my old life back in San Francisco. But this time I wanted to do it all myself. I was tired of hiring people to do things for me. I was tired of sitting behind a screen all day and most of the night and not having anything physical, other than money, to show for myself at the end of it all. I wanted the bungalow project to be all mine. I wanted to really earn the money that would finally come when I could sell it for a profit.

Refurbishing this place was going to be a lot more work than I'd imagined, though. No doubt about it.

My plan was to spend a little time regrouping, work to get the bungalow in prime shape, sell the place, and move back to the city and find a new job with a new law firm. I figured six months would do the trick. I could go back in the summer when things were in a lull. I had no doubt that with my education and my resume, I would be able to find another job in no time. And with the money from selling a freshly renovated beach house and from my divorce, I should be able to find myself a new place back in the city with little problem.

Shorty finished his breakfast and hopped into the wide front window to clean himself and watch the world go by. I reached into the fridge and pulled out the chocolate croissant I'd bought from the coffee shop the night before. I heated it in the microwave for a couple of seconds to take the refrigerator chill off. It was a little stale, but the chocolate oozed as I bit into it and the flakes covered my mouth and coat and I laughed as I brushed them off.

A memory of rolling out croissants with my grandmother flashed into my head. She'd owned a bakery when I was young and I'd spent summers with her, baking cupcakes and cookies and serving customers in her sunny store in Alabama.

Her croissants were much better than the one I was currently eating. I wondered if there was a bakery in town and, if so, whether it was open and serving croissants.

When I finished eating the mediocre breakfast, I washed up and made a grocery list. I would need some serious supplies if I planned to stay here and clean the place up. Then I got dressed quickly, pulled back my dark curls into a messy ponytail, threw just enough makeup on to feel presentable, and grabbed my list. But as I looked outside, what I really wanted to do was go for a walk down to the boardwalk. I wanted to explore our new home. And I wanted some time to meander and think.

"You up for a walk, Shorty old boy?" I said.

Shorty sat in the window and flicked his tail. I knew he wanted to explore, too. After I finished my coffee, I slipped on my jacket and nodded to him, then grabbed my keys. He was the kind of cat who I didn't have to worry about. He liked to stay near me at all times, so I knew we could take a stroll and I wouldn't lose him.

The breeze was chilly but invigorating as we set out. Some of my hope returned as we walked down to the boardwalk. Maybe this move wasn't the worst decision I ever made after all.

Moonstone Bay had that effortless charm you only find in coastal towns, with its narrow streets lined by weathered but cheerful shops. Each storefront had a bit of personality—a painted sign here, a potted plant there—and the few people out this early gave friendly nods as they passed. The salt-tinged air mingled with the faint aroma of coffee from a nearby cafe, and I felt that unmistakable pull of a place that could start to feel like home. I followed Shorty, who seemed to know exactly where he was headed, despite the fact that I'd never brought him to Moonstone Bay before.

We hit the boardwalk ten minutes later. Because it was

February, the place was largely deserted, although I noticed a diner on the far right that seemed to be doing a brisk business. I'd have to check it out at some point.

The boardwalk stretched out in front of us, quiet and a little rough around the edges. Salt-stained planks led the way past closed-up souvenir stalls and weathered benches. The whole scene washed in the soft gray of a foggy morning. The waves rolled in lazily nearby, filling the air with the steady hush of the ocean.

Shorty, in his element, strutted ahead with the confidence of a cat who owned the place. I followed, my steps crunching lightly on the sandy pavement that skirted the boardwalk. I pulled my jacket a bit tighter around me, feeling the chill carried on the ocean breeze.

The few shops that stood at the beach end of the boardwalk were mostly closed. I walked past several tourist places with souvenirs for sale, a real estate office and nail salon, along with a couple of bars, all closed.

A seagull landed a few feet down the boardwalk, eyeing Shorty with a mix of curiosity and caution. "Don't even think about it," I warned the bird, half-joking.

I thought he might lunge for the squawking gull, but instead, he turned toward one of the shops to the left of us like a cat on a mission. Without a second thought, he slipped through the partially open door, and I hurried to catch up with him.

"Shorty! Hey!" I bit my lip and peered in the door.

I hesitated for another few seconds and looked around the outside of the place. A sign hung in the window that said "Rinaldi Investigations." Beneath it hung a second sign, one that was handwritten in a sloppy sloping print. "Space for Lease. Inquire Inside." I frowned. The window was dusty, and there was a crack in one of the panes. The place almost seemed abandoned, and it made me deeply uncomfortable to go after Shorty. But I couldn't leave him there.

Finally, I took a deep breath and pushed through the partially open door in search of my cat.

2

The door caught on something as I pushed it open and I had to shove hard to get inside. Once I did, I saw Shorty near the back of the long, rectangular space. He was being pet by a man who'd stooped to run his hand along my cat's back.

When the man heard the door, he turned his head toward me. Our eyes met, and I sucked in a breath, feeling a spark pass from the top of my head to the tip of my toes. *He's the one.*

What? I had no idea where the words had come from, but as they floated around my mind, they washed over me with such certainty that I shook my head a little.

I lost all sense of myself and my surroundings as the man gave me a smile and then straightened and walked toward me. He wore a wrinkled light blue polo shirt and jeans. The blue of his shirt set off the most incredibly deep blue eyes I'd ever seen. He had a strong jaw and thick brown hair. I knew I was smiling at him like a goofball, but I couldn't help the grin that spread across my face. What on earth was happening to me?

"Hey, there," he said as he held out his hand. It was strong and his nails were well manicured, despite the otherwise disheveled look of him. Shorty meowed loudly as he came along and watched the two of us. I ignored him completely and held the man's hand a beat too long.

"Vince Rinaldi. Were you here about the lease?" he asked.

I stumbled over my words, not understanding him, completely befuddled.

"Lease? No..." I looked down at Shorty, who sat at our feet swishing his tail, watching our conversation. Almost as if he'd set the whole thing up, scoundrel. "No, I just followed my cat."

"Oh, right. Chicken Wing."

"No, Shortcake."

He cocked an eyebrow at me and laughed. "Oh, I named him Chicken Wing last night. We shared a couple while I was... out..."

"You must be thinking of a different cat. We just got into town last night."

"It was pretty late," he said with a laugh.

"I don't think so. He was with me all night."

"Alright. Maybe. So you aren't here about the lease, then?" His face fell, and he ran a hand through his already messy hair. I had an almost overwhelming urge to reach out and fix it for him.

I thought back to that sign in the window. "You're leasing this place out?" I arched my eyebrows and looked around a little more closely.

The office had seen better days. Dusty sunlight filtered through grimy windows, casting hazy squares onto a faded carpet that had probably once been beige, but now looked more like a patchwork of coffee stains and scuff marks. A single desk stood near the back, cluttered with old files and a half-empty coffee cup, its corner chipped and sagging slightly. The walls were a dingy off-white, lined with peeling edges of wallpaper that hinted at a different era. Despite the gloom, I could see a lot of potential—polished up with new paint, light flooding in through sparkling windows. It was rough, no question, but it had the bones of something wonderful.

"Yep, need to lease the place out. Or part of it, anyway." He turned away from me and put his hands in the pockets of his slacks. "I want to keep a desk here for my P.I. business, so whoever leases the place will have to agree to that, but I've got to lease the rest out. Can't afford to keep it otherwise."

"You own it?"

He nodded. "It was my parents' place. My dad's shop. They gave it to me when they...passed."

"Oh, I'm sorry," I told him.

"Don't worry, it was a while ago," he replied and then bent down and ran his hand along Shorty's back. The cat meowed and wound his body around him as I looked around the room.

I scanned the space as he talked and for some reason, the summers at my grandmother's bakery popped into my head again. My mind flashed back to how happy everyone in town had always been to see her when they came into her shop, how delicious it smelled, how fun it had been to decorate cookies and stand behind the counter ringing people up. Visiting her and helping her in her bakery were some of my happiest times as an otherwise unhappy child. And scanning this empty space full of dust and cobwebs, I had a sudden image flash in front of me of this space as a cozy bakery where people came to meet, to enjoy treats, to gather together. The place is happy and clean and full of people. Not dejected like it currently was.

"How much?" I asked.

"How much what?" Vince replied, stooping even more to scratch Shorty's face as Shorty leaned in.

"How much are you charging? For rent?"

He stood and gazed at me for a beat longer. Those blue eyes bored into my soul and I blushed.

"Two thousand a month with a month's rent deposit. One year contract."

"And you want to keep part of it to run a private investigating business out of? Don't you think that's a little...odd?"

He shrugged. "Probably. But I don't have a lot of options, lady. I need to run my business still. Can't very well do that out of a car. At least I don't think I can." He frowned as if considering it.

"What about a bakery?"

He turned his frown on me, eyebrows raised. "Here? I mean, it's possible. You'd have to do some...renovating, I would imagine. It'd be a little...odd...with a P.I. business."

I gave a little laugh, glancing around at the space with fresh eyes. "Maybe. But that's part of the charm, don't you think? People love a quirky place with a story."

Vince seemed to consider this, then shrugged. "Guess I never thought of it that way. Most people just want something new and shiny these days." He tilted his head at me, a hint of curiosity in his expression. "You're serious, though? About the bakery?"

"I'll take it," I said, surprising myself *and* him. Shorty and Vince stared at me, both a little stunned, and I blushed. "I'll take it for a bakery."

Vince grinned, something almost boyish about the way his eyes lit up. "Okay," he said, rubbing the back of his neck. "Yeah, I can see it. Sure. Let me just go get some, uh, paperwork..."

3

Fifteen minutes later, Shorty and I walked out the front door of the space, me with a lease in hand, and Shorty licking his lips after Vince's offering of pieces from a leftover chicken wing. What on earth had I just done? I couldn't believe myself. It almost felt as though I'd been under a magic spell while inside that space. As soon as I left, I shivered and started to regret everything.

But this time, I was going to follow through with my gut. And my gut was telling me that I was supposed to set up a bakery in that crumbling office space. I tried hard not to think about my original plan, the one where I came to Moonstone Bay to fix the bungalow up, sold it for a lot of cash, and then jetted off back to the big city. Clearly, the bakery idea wasn't going to fit nicely into that plan.

But I would deal with that later.

For now, I stopped by the small grocery store off the highway and bought sustenance for Shorty and I—a loaf of bread and cheese and ham, eggs for the morning, coffee and a coffeepot, cat food, and a cord of wood. The bungalow had a small fireplace, and I hoped that the thing wasn't too neglected so that I could make myself a nice fire to keep warm. I'd have to call someone to fix the heater soon.

Which reminded me, I wanted to get someone over to the shop—I was already calling it the shop in my mind—soon to give me estimates on renovating the place to build it out as a bakery. I had no idea what that would entail, how much I would need to scrape together from my divorce settlement, or how long the whole thing would take to get going, but I was ready to find out.

After putting away groceries, feeding Shorty, and throwing together a quick dinner, I made myself a cup of tea and then looked over the few boxes I'd brought with me, knowing that somewhere in there was my grandmother's old recipe book. She'd given it to me just before she'd died, and it was one of the few things I'd kept from my childhood. It took three tries, but I finally found the box with papers, books, and other office supplies. Digging through, I finally unearthed the old recipe binder, its once-bright red cover faded to a soft, dusty pink. The edges were frayed, and the plastic sleeves holding the hand-written recipe cards had yellowed with age. My grandmother's looping cursive was visible through the cloudy plastic, the words "Mona's Specials" written with the same care she'd put into every pie crust she ever made.

Shortcake pawed at the edge of the box, his green eyes locked on the binder as if he sensed its importance. "What's this?" I asked him with a chuckle, holding the book up for him to inspect. He sniffed delicately at the corner before letting out a decisive meow, as if to give his approval.

I set the book aside for a moment as a shiver passed through me and decided to try out the bungalow's fireplace before digging into recipes. The room was chilly, and I was already bundled up in a sweater and a thick pair of socks, but a fire felt like the perfect finishing touch for my first real night in the place.

As I added some logs to the old fireplace, I thought about just how far the bungalow was from the polished, pristine apartment I'd left behind in San Francisco. The heater didn't work; the sink dripped incessantly, the curtains were practically cobweb collectors, and every corner seemed to have its own layer of dust. I'd definitely need an arsenal of cleaning supplies and maybe a professional exterminator. Shorty gave a little meow as he watched me, and I nodded my head in agreement. We were in trouble.

And as I added a few crumpled pieces of newspaper under the logs, the insanity of my decision hit me and I sat back on my heels, staring into space. What was I even doing? Opening a bakery in a town I barely knew, with no practical knowledge of how to run one, and only the faintest memories of summers baking with my grandmother. What did I even need to start a bakery? An oven, sure, but beyond that...? This whole plan seemed impulsive at best and downright ridiculous at worst.

I couldn't wait to hear what mother thought of my plan. No doubt she would call it reckless, if not outright absurd. If she even heard about it... I wondered suddenly as I leaned back in and lit the paper. Could I keep it from her, at least until I had something to show for it?

Probably not, but it was a nice thought.

As if summoned by my musings, my phone buzzed in my lap. I glanced down. Speak of the devil—or rather, Mother. I sighed and picked up.

"Hi, Mom." I stretched my hands out to the small fire I'd managed to coax to life, feeling warmth finally creep into my fingers. I took a sip of my tea, letting myself sink back into the deep scratchiness of the couch. It felt a bit like sitting on a pile of hay, but for now, it was mine.

"Virginia! Thank goodness. I was sure you'd gone missing in that little town," she said, sounding exasperated.

I rolled my eyes, a half-smile tugging at my lips. "Mom, it's not exactly the wilderness. I'm a mile from a grocery store and ten minutes from a coffee shop."

"Oh, honey, that's what people always say right before they're eaten by wolves or run out of town by some shady character," she said, her tone both dismissive and vaguely ominous. "If I hadn't gotten through, I was going to call the Moonstone Bay police. I have them saved as a contact now!"

"Well, that's a relief." I stifled a laugh and glanced at Shorty, who twitched his tail as if to say *you should've expected this.* "Mom, I'm fine. Really. I even figured out how to start a fire—all by myself." I stretched my legs, feeling oddly proud and very much at home, despite the lumps in the old sofa.

There was a beat of silence before her voice softened, slipping from her usual theatrics to a gentle chiding. "You know, I still don't understand why you needed to go so far, Virginia. You could have come home for a few weeks. Daddy and I wouldn't have minded, honey. We know you'll get your act together. We had such great plans for you. You just need to buck up, I think."

I sighed, rubbing Shorty's back. "I know, Mom. But those plans didn't really turn out, did they?" I took another sip of tea and stared at the fire, half-wishing she could see the cozy scene, even though I knew she'd probably just find more to complain about.

"Well, you didn't need to go all the way out there. It feels like you're running away."

I had nothing to say to that and so I let the discomforting quiet stretch out, knowing she would fill it before too long.

"Are you going to practice law while you're out there? Or are you planning to just loaf around?"

I held my breath, then decided to let myself be bold. "You

know, I've actually been thinking about Grandma's bakery a lot. Remember all those summers? The croissants, her cookies?"

"Oh, Virginia, that was ages ago! And besides, we were practically living on fumes back then. I don't know why you'd bring that up."

I chewed on my lip, deciding it best to not say another thing about the bakery idea. As I tried to figure out a response, I looked around the little bungalow. It may have been held together with spiderwebs and a healthy layer of dust, but the fire crackled invitingly, and Shorty was purring beside me. "I don't know. Just wondering, I guess."

Finally, her voice softened again, this time with a rare warmth. "Is this about Valentine's Day? I know it's probably not going to be an easy day for you. Do you want to come back and have lunch with me? You can bring Shorty, have Daddy watch him," she said.

It was only then that I realized tomorrow would be my first Valentine's Day after the divorce. I took a big gulp of tea, and suddenly all the excitement of my new dreams fell flat, like a soufflé that had been jiggled too much.

"No, I need to stay here. Thanks, though," I replied.

We were both quiet for a moment, and I felt a pang of homesickness, or maybe just regret. It seemed my mother was determined not to understand this part of me, the part that wanted something smaller, something simpler.

"Well, call me tomorrow, at least. Alright?"

I hung up and glanced at the old recipe book before I stared at the fire a while longer. All energy for recipe research had drained out of me and I pushed the old book aside for another day. Shorty jumped up and sat on my lap. At least we had each other, I consoled myself.

And at least I had a new dream to occupy my mind.

4

The next morning, after a quick cereal and coffee breakfast, I left Shorty at the bungalow to go meet a contractor I'd contacted the evening before over at the shop. The cat sat in the window flicking his tail in judgement as I locked him in.

"Sorry," I mouthed to him with a little wave. He turned away and looked out the other side of the window. Served me right, I supposed. I knew he would want to join me, but I needed to concentrate so he would have to stay home.

I'd texted Vince about the meeting the night before but hadn't heard back from him. I hoped he'd gotten the message because he hadn't given me keys yet. I was already having serious misgivings about this arrangement for sharing the space with him. Maybe I should've looked for another place to make a bakery, one that made more sense and one that didn't come with an attractive but unkempt private detective.

Nah. As much as I hated to admit it, I thought that Vince might be part of the draw of the place. Despite my recent divorce and despite the fact that the man seemed to be a serious mess, there was something about him I couldn't shake.

Walking along the boardwalk, I took in the quiet charm of Moonstone Bay in the off-season. The morning was sunny but brisk, and a few shop owners setting up for the day gave me friendly nods and waves. I smiled back, feeling a small flutter of anticipation at the idea of becoming part of this little community. Soon enough, I'd know their names, their stories—and they'd be my neighbors once I had the bakery up and running. I could already picture the place: gleaming glass counters filled with pastries, a cozy corner with tables, maybe even a chalkboard menu with rotating daily specials. Still, a little worry niggled at me. The boardwalk seemed quiet now, and it was the middle of winter. Would there be enough foot traffic here year-round to keep a bakery afloat? Or would I be baking for an empty shop?

Something glinted on the boardwalk as I approached the space I'd leased the day before, and I realized as I got closer that it was broken glass. I slowed, my pulse picking up as I saw shards littering the ground in front of the window. My frown deepened as I realized that someone had broken a pane of glass in the front window. What could have happened? I remembered it being cracked the day before, but this looked like someone smashed into the glass with a lot of force very recently.

"Yikes," a voice set behind me a minute later as I stood assessing the damage.

I turned quickly and saw a woman in overalls and a bright red flannel shirt with a utility belt slung confidently around her waist. She was shorter than me by at least half a foot, with a sturdy, curvy frame that seemed perfect for hefting hammers or tackling drywall. Her round face, framed by a messy ponytail, lit up with a friendly grin that hinted at a wicked sense of humor lurking just beneath the surface.

"Hey, I'm Lois Wheeler," she said and stuck out her hand.

I shook it with a smile. "I'm Ginny Malone. I'm the one who called you about renovating this place."

She nodded. "I figured. It's a small town. You kinda stand out."

I grinned. "Hey, I like your name. I've never met a Lois before."

She shrugged. "My dad has a thing for superman." She turned to look at the outside of Vince's place and frowned when she noticed the broken pane. "You know what happened here?"

I shrugged, crossing my arms and looking back at the mess. "It wasn't like this yesterday," I said, feeling a twinge of unease as I thought about my decision to lease the place. "Do you get a lot of crime around here?"

Lois let out a little huff of a laugh, but her expression stayed serious as she studied the glass. "Not usually, no. Pretty quiet, actually." She shot me a knowing look. "This isn't exactly what you signed up for, huh?"

I bit my lip, the excitement I'd felt the day before wobbling a little. "Not at all. But maybe it's just a... random accident? Maybe a seagull got bold," I suggested, forcing a small laugh.

Lois smiled, but her eyes lingered on the glass a beat longer before she looked back at me. "The door's open. Should we go inside and see what's up?"

Sure enough, the door was slightly open, just how I'd found it yesterday. I hoped it wasn't some sort of structural issue and that the door actually closed and locked without trouble. I raised my eyebrows.

"Oh, yeah, sure." I pushed the door open and more glass fell out of the pane, crunching on the ground at my feet. I stepped over the mess the best I could.

The musty smell hit me first, followed by something metallic that made my stomach churn. As my eyes adjusted to the dim interior, I saw a figure sprawled face-down on the floor.

My heart leapt into my throat. "Vince?" I called out, my voice shaky. The sound of my own voice was loud in the silence, as if the room had been holding its breath.

No response.

Lois moved closer, then suddenly backed away, her face pale. "That's not Vince," she said, her voice tight. "But whoever it is, they're not breathing."

I felt the room spin, a wave of nausea hitting me as I forced myself to look closer. The still form on the floor, the angle of the body—it was all wrong. What am I even doing here? I came to plan out a bakery, not... this.

I fumbled for my phone, my hands shaking as I dialed 911. "There's been a... a shooting, I think," I managed to say when the operator answered. "At Rinaldi Investigations on the board-walk. Please hurry."

As I gave them the address, I couldn't tear my eyes away from the still form on the floor. What had I gotten myself into?

5

As we waited for the police to arrive, I found myself cataloging details of the scene, my lawyer's mind kicking into gear despite the shock. The victim was male, middle-aged from what I could tell. His right hand was outstretched, fingers curled slightly around a hammer, of all things.

A small pool of blood had formed under him, and I quickly averted my eyes, focusing instead on the surroundings. The back of his jacket was torn and stained, and I caught a glimpse of what looked like a small, dark hole just below his shoulder blade. Gunshot wound, I thought. Judging by the angle of his body, it seemed as if he'd been turned toward the wall when he was shot in the back, so he had likely been surprised by his attacker.

Lois bent over to get a closer look, her expression grim. She gave a short, decisive nod. "Yep. He looks like a goner," she said, straightening up and wiping her hands on her overalls, though she hadn't touched anything. The words were matter-of-fact, but I saw a flicker of unease in her eyes. "Wonder if that hammer was what broke the window? Although, why break the window if the door's wide open?"

I'd wondered the same things. It didn't make a lot of sense any way I looked at it.

"Do you recognize him?" I asked Lois, my voice barely above a whisper.

She shook her head, her gaze darting from the body to the door, as if hoping for an escape route. "There's something familiar about him but...no, not from this angle. He doesn't look local. Too... polished, you know?"

I nodded, feeling a strange mixture of dread and curiosity building in my chest. Why the hammer? And why had he been killed here of all places? Had Vince had something to do with it? The thought sent a chill down my spine.

The wail of sirens pierced the air, growing louder as they approached. Moments later, heavy footsteps thundered on the boardwalk. "In here!" I called out.

A tall, broad-shouldered man in a khaki uniform appeared in the doorway, his hand resting on his holstered gun. "I'm Sheriff Donovan," he announced, his eyes quickly surveying the scene. "Which one of you ladies called this in?"

"I did," I said, stepping forward. "I'm Virginia Malone. I just moved to town."

Lois stepped forward as well, and nodded her head at him. "Sheriff, good to see you."

"Howdy, Lois," he said as he glanced at the body on the floor. He motioned for two officers behind him to step inside, and they moved quickly and started collecting evidence.

Sheriff Donovan's gaze moved from me to the body on the floor, his expression growing more serious. "Alright, Ms. Malone, can you tell me what you found when you came in?" he asked, his voice steady but laced with authority.

"I was supposed to meet Lois," I said, nodding at Lois, "and as we got here, we noticed the broken glass." I pointed toward the shattered window. "When we walked in, we found...him." I motioned toward the body, the weight of the situation settling on me as I spoke. "I don't know who he is."

He gave a slow nod, taking notes. "And you didn't see anyone else in the area? Anyone suspicious hanging around this morning?"

"No one," I replied, glancing at Lois, who nodded in agreement. "It was quiet when we got here."

The sheriff's eyes narrowed, as if weighing my answer. "And why were you ladies meeting here?"

I blushed, feeling the words come out awkwardly. "I just signed a lease yesterday, with Vince Rinaldi. He—he was supposed to be here, too. He owns the place, as far as I know."

Sheriff Donovan scribbled something in his notepad, then looked up, his gaze sharp. "Vince Rinaldi, huh?" He gave a dry, humorless smile. "Can't say I'm surprised."

Before I could ask what he meant, a soft groan came from behind the rickety partition near an old desk in the back of the store. The sheriff's expression hardened, and he signaled for one of the officers to follow as he approached the source of the noise. A second later, his face shifted to something between irritation and disbelief as he put his hands on his hips and sighed.

"Rinaldi! Get your sorry behind out here!" he barked.

Another groan, followed by the sound of something—or someone—stumbling against furniture. The partition wobbled, and suddenly Vince appeared, looking disheveled and distinctly green around the gills.

"What's your problem now, Donovan? I didn't say you could come in here. What is this? Illegal search and seizure?" Vince slurred, then blinked and stopped talking as he registered the scene before him.

The sheriff's jaw clenched. "My problem, Rinaldi, is the

dead body in your shop. Care to explain why you're passed out drunk while there's a murder victim on your floor?"

Vince's eyes widened as he processed the sheriff's words. He stumbled forward, trying to see around the partition. "Dead body? What are you talking about?"

Sheriff Donovan blocked his view, his voice dripping with sarcasm. "Oh, I'm sorry. Did I interrupt your beauty sleep? Were you here all night, or is this just your usual morning routine?"

Vince glared at the sheriff, though the effect was somewhat dampened by his obvious hangover. "Yeah, I was here. Working late. Had a drink. Or two."

"And you didn't hear anything unusual? No gunshot? No struggle? Or were you too busy playing detective to notice a real crime?"

The color drained from Vince's face as the gravity of the situation seemed to hit him finally. "No, I... I didn't hear anything. I swear!"

"You slept through a man being murdered? How much did you have to drink, son?" the sheriff asked, his tone a mixture of disgust and disbelief.

"It's Valentine's Day!"

Clearly, the sheriff was as puzzled as I was what that had to do with the situation at hand.

"I'm not following," he said.

Vince blushed and kicked at the empty liquor bottle on the floor near him. It made a harsh clanging noise. "I mean, I only planned to have a couple...Things maybe got a little out of hand."

The sheriff eyed him for a long moment before he said, "what I'm hearing is, you were drunk as a skunk. And you don't have an alibi."

Vince frowned. But he nodded as he looked down at his tennis shoes.

The sheriff sighed and put his hands on his hips, looking around the dirty space. Then he turned to me. "And you two just happened to show up to have a meeting and find this man?"

I nodded. "Yes, sir."

"Why were you here again?"

"I rented this space from Mr. Rinaldi," I said again, trying not to show my frustration with having to repeat my story. I knew he was just trying to connect important dots. "I was here to meet the contractor. We're going to start a bakery." I couldn't keep the excitement from my voice.

The sheriff's eyebrows shot up, and he looked around again. "Here? A bakery?"

I heard the skepticism in his voice, and immediately my cheeks burned.

Lois chimed in. "Oh, for sure, Sheriff. Some counter space here," she said, motioning toward the same place I'd imagined a counter. "Plenty of room for some bakery cases. Commercial ovens in the back, over that a way. Would hardly take any work at all," she said matter-of-factly, crossing her arms over her large chest.

I couldn't help but grin. This was a woman after my own heart and in that moment, even before I'd heard her plan or her prices, I decided I would hire her to make this bakery dream come true. "Some new flooring and a little bit of cleaning will round it all out," I added. "We'll have some tables in front for customers who want to sit and enjoy the view out that big window." The big, currently cracked window. I didn't want to have to pay for the repairs, but it would be something to haggle over with Vince later. He seemed up to his eyeballs in worry at present.

"Well, that's an interesting idea, ma'am," the sheriff

responded finally, after eyeing us both like he was worried for our sanity. Then he turned back to Vince.

"Look, the long and short of it is that you don't have an alibi, son. And you own the building. In my book, that makes you mighty suspicious. Were you here all night, Mr. Rinaldi?"

"Come on, I don't know anything and you and I both know that! I know what you're trying to do, Donovan. It's not going to work. What's the motive?"

My heart rate went through the roof watching the exchange. I had no idea what to think. Vince didn't seem like the type who would murder someone. He was a wreck. There was no doubt about that. But I doubted he was a murderer. Still, the sheriff had a point about the alibi.

Suddenly Vince made a face, and he crouched down to stare at the body. I hoped he wasn't going to puke.

"Wait a minute," Vince said, his voice hoarse. "I know this guy. It's Marcus Holloway. We went to high school together."

"I knew he looked familiar!" Lois exclaimed.

A second officer who'd been walking through the space suddenly called out. "Donovan, you need to see this."

Sheriff Donovan moved to where Vince had been sleeping and I moved closer too, suddenly desperately curious to know what they'd found.

On the ground near Vince's desk was a gun.

He turned to address all of us. "Alright, folks. This is an active crime scene. I need everyone to clear out so we can process the area. Ms. Malone, Ms. Wheeler, I'll be in touch to get your official statements. And Mr. Rinaldi, you're coming with me."

The sheriff pulled out a set of handcuffs and Vince got even more green around the gills.

"You have to believe me. I didn't do this," he said as the sheriff slapped the cuffs on him and angled him out the door.

As he passed me, our eyes met and the pleading look he sent me melted my heart. I wasn't sure if he was a criminal or not, but I meant to find out.

6

"Wow. That was crazy," Lois said as we stepped into the late morning sunshine. "Need a reset?"

"I could definitely use one," I replied with a shaky smile.

She checked her watch. "Perfect timing. How about breakfast at Moonstone Diner? We can talk over the bakery plans while I grab a bite before my next meeting."

"Sounds great."

The bell above the door jingled as we stepped into Moonstone Diner and I was immediately grateful for the warmth. The restaurant was crowded, nearly every booth and seat filled. Lois waved at people she knew, and I got a lot of stares.

The place was an eclectic mix of beach-town charm and no-nonsense grit, with driftwood signs on the walls and mismatched, colorful chairs scattered across the room. A sun-worn, silver-haired woman with a faded denim apron glanced up from behind the counter and narrowed her eyes at us.

"Lois," she called out, her eyes twinkling, "you brought a fresh face." She looked me over with mock suspicion. "City girl, huh?"

Lois laughed and introduced me. "Fran, this is Ginny. Ginny, this is Fran. She owns the diner. Ginny's new in town—and opening a bakery."

Fran raised an eyebrow. "Well, you'd better know what you're doing. And don't get any ideas about cutting into my business," she said with a playful smirk. "You all take that booth over there. I'll be by with coffee."

Lois leaned over to me as we walked toward the booth. "Fran's one of a kind. She's the unofficial mayor around here and knows everything about everyone." She gave me a knowing grin. "Stick around long enough, and she'll probably keep tabs on you, too."

Was that a good thing? I couldn't tell. But I suddenly worried about whether we'd be competing for customers. By the look of the packed diner and the way Fran was yacking it up with the patrons, I wouldn't stand a chance against her.

As we walked to our booth, a few locals offered friendly nods and curious glances. One man leaned back in his chair and called out, "Lois! Everything alright over at Vince's?"

"Just a little excitement," Lois replied, keeping her tone light. "You'll have to ask Sheriff Donovan if you want any more than that."

The man grumbled, but Lois ignored it as we settled into the booth. Sunlight streamed through the large window beside us, illuminating the chalkboard menu scrawled in colorful, uneven handwriting. It listed everything from Fran's Famous Pancakes to Seafood Omelets to Chowder in a Bread Bowl—a true mix of diner staples and local twists. The place felt worn but loved, like it had absorbed years of conversations, laughter, and a healthy dose of gossip.

"Don't worry," Lois said, catching my eye as I glanced at the menu. "Fran's diner isn't anything like a bakery. You two will be just fine coexisting on the boardwalk."

I laughed, relaxing a bit. "Good to know. I had a moment of panic, thinking I'd just signed up for a turf war."

"No way," Lois replied with a grin. "Fran's all bark and no bite... unless you mess with her salt-and-pepper shakers. Then you're on your own."

Fran strode over as if she knew we were talking about her, notepad in hand. She gave us a pointed look, as if daring us to order anything complicated.

"Well? What'll it be?" she asked, raising an eyebrow.

Lois didn't even look at the menu. "The usual, Fran. Blueberry pancakes, extra crispy bacon."

Fran jotted it down with a nod and turned to me, her sharp eyes appraising. "And you?"

I glanced at the options, feeling slightly on the spot. "Just scrambled eggs and toast, please. And coffee."

"Just eggs and toast?" she repeated, her voice laced with mild disappointment, as if I'd passed up a chance at culinary greatness. "Suit yourself." She scribbled it down, and I caught the hint of a smirk. "Suit yourself, city girl."

As soon as Fran walked away, Lois leaned back, giving me a wry smile. "So," she said, her eyes twinkling. "You met Vince. What do you think?"

I laughed, feeling a little blush creep up. "Honestly? He's... rough around the edges. Kind of charming, but not exactly polished."

Lois nodded, a knowing grin tugging at her lips. "Yep, that's Vince. Grew up right here in Moonstone Bay, big Italian family and all. We were in the same grade. Good guy at heart, just... let's say, life hasn't been too gentle with him." She paused, her expression softening. "His parents passed away when we were seniors, and he inherited the shop. I don't think he ever really knew what to do with himself after that."

I listened, feeling a pang of sympathy for him. "That must've been tough."

"It was," Lois said, her tone turning a little wistful. "He stuck around, though. Married a few years back, but his wife left him last year. Since then... well, I guess you could say he's become a bit of a local character. He's always had a knack for finding trouble, but now... now he's more likely to be found sleeping it off than solving it."

I raised an eyebrow, both surprised and amused. "Not exactly the sharp-eyed detective type, then?"

Lois chuckled, shaking her head. "Not even close. Mostly folks around here hire him for small stuff—lost dogs, missing keys, the occasional cheating partner. He's good enough for that, and no one minds giving him work just to help him get by." She paused, leaning in with a mischievous glint in her eye. "Plus, I think half the town keeps hoping he'll finally pull himself together. He's like that stray dog you can't quite bring yourself to shoo away."

Just as I was about to ask more about Vince's family, Fran returned, balancing our plates with a proud grin. She set Lois's blueberry pancakes down, and I noticed they were sprinkled with powdered sugar and decorated with a dollop of whipped cream shaped into a little heart.

My eggs and toast arrived with a small chocolate on the side, wrapped in foil, with a heart on it. Fran caught my look and raised an eyebrow, daring me to comment. "You can blame Marvin for the Valentine's flair." She jerked her thumb over her shoulder, and the cook—a stocky, bashful man with a streak of gray in his hair—leaned out from the kitchen window to give us a shy wave.

"I think it's adorable," I said, smiling at both of them. "Thanks, Marvin!"

Fran smirked, muttering, "Yeah, well, don't go spreading it

around that we're getting soft in here." She turned with a wink and sauntered back to the counter.

I took a bite of the eggs, and despite their simplicity, they were cooked perfectly—soft and buttery, with just the right amount of salt. I glanced over at Fran, who had returned to her post at the counter, and saw the faintest look of satisfaction in her eyes as she watched me enjoy it.

As we ate, Lois leaned back in the booth and gave me an appraising look. "So, where are you from? What brought you to Moonstone Bay, anyway? This place isn't exactly the spot for city folks looking to keep busy."

I took a sip of my coffee, wondering how much to share. "I'm from San Francisco, born and raised," I said, deciding to keep it simple. "So not too far. I just needed... a change, I guess. A little distance to get my head clear."

Lois nodded, and I could tell she understood without needing the details. "San Francisco, huh? No wonder you look so put together. The real question, though, is do you know what you're getting yourself into? I mean, renovating that shop isn't going to be the easiest project, even on a good day. And I hate to say it, but I'm expecting surprises. I love Vince like a brother, but somehow I doubt he's been taking excellent care of that building over the past dozen years."

I shrugged, feeling heat creep into my face as I thought not only of the bakery project that was now completely up in the air, but also of my dilapidated bungalow. What would Lois think if she knew about the bungalow?

"You know what? Don't worry about it," Lois said with an easy smile. "I've got loads of experience, and this thing will be a breeze. Although you might need to do a little bit of hands-on work to get your bakery off the ground."

I laughed, feeling a bit more at ease. "Oh, believe me, I'm ready for hands-on work. I've spent way too many years behind a desk for my own sanity. Hands-on is exactly what I was hoping for." And as I said it, I realized just how true it was. I couldn't wait to get my hands dirty with all the fixing-up that waited in my future.

"Yeah? What kind of desk work are we talking about here?" Lois asked, curiosity sparking in her eyes.

"Lawyer," I said, shrugging. "But I'm taking a break for now. No courtrooms or clients for me for a while." I saw her eyes widen a bit, but thankfully, she didn't press.

"I can respect that," Lois said. "Everybody needs a break now and then." She finished off her pancakes and leaned back, giving me a satisfied nod. "So, now that you've signed the lease with Vince, any ideas on how you want this bakery set up? Ovens, counters, all that?"

I pulled out my notebook, showing her some rough sketches. "I'd love a welcoming setup with open counters and maybe a small seating area by the window. Nothing too fancy, just cozy and warm. I liked everything you told the sheriff back there."

Lois nodded. "Got it. I'll start with the essentials—ovens, counters, whatever permits we need. I'll scope out the place once the sheriff's done poking around and get a sense of what we're working with." She shrugged, tucking her notebook away. "It's a small town, so the building permits shouldn't be too bad. As long as we keep it simple, I can probably get started this week. Assuming..."

I nodded, knowing exactly what she was assuming. Assuming Vince Rinaldi wasn't a murderer. Assuming the police would finish their investigation and that the space would be open to us again soon. Assuming no other surprises waited for us.

I felt my excitement bubbling up, grateful for her easygoing approach. "Sounds perfect. And if you have any questions about the layout or need me to make a decision, just let me know."

She gave me a thumbs-up. "You got it."

Just as Lois and I were finishing up, Fran appeared at our table, the check in hand. She set it down and leaned in slightly, her expression sharp with curiosity.

"So," she said, her voice low but pointed, "heard things got a little dramatic over at Rinaldi's this morning. What's the story?"

Lois hesitated for only a second before sighing. "Someone died, Fran. Over at the shop."

Fran's eyebrows shot up. "Died? Who?"

"Marcus Holloway," Lois replied, watching Fran closely. "You remember him?"

Fran scoffed, crossing her arms. "Oh, I remember him, alright. That boy was nothing but trouble back in the day. It's too bad, but I can't say I'm shocked he ended up the way he did." She shook her head and frowned, her curiosity replaced by something softer. "What was he even doing back here? Haven't seen him around Moonstone Bay in a decade or more."

"No idea," Lois said, her tone neutral, though her expression darkened.

"You don't think it has anything to do with Alma, does it?" Fran asked, raising her eyebrows.

Lois frowned and shrugged.

I glanced between them, intrigued by who Alma might be. It seemed important, but I didn't want to interrupt.

Fran clicked her tongue, then leaned in closer. "You two listen to me. Stay out of whatever this is, you hear me? Nothing good comes from sticking your nose in someone else's mess." Her eyes softened just a bit as she looked between us. "I know trouble when I see it, and I'd rather not see either of you caught up in it. You stay safe, alright?"

I smiled, warmed by the concern under her gruff exterior. "We will, Fran. Promise."

After we paid our bill, Lois gave me a small, wry smile. "I knew it wouldn't take her long to come fishing for info. Fran is always in the thick of it."

"Who is Alma?" I asked as I put my wallet back in my purse and prepared to leave.

Lois' face turned dark. "Alma was a girl I went to high school with. She disappeared right before graduation. Old sad things best left in the past," Lois said as she stood. Before I could ask anything else, she said, "Alright, ready to face the world again?"

I nodded, filing the story of Alma away for later. "Ready as I'll ever be," I replied, grabbing my bag.

We stood, leaving the warmth of the diner behind as we stepped toward the door, the weight of Fran's warning still lingering in the back of my mind.

7

As we stepped outside, the boardwalk buzzed with energy, the calm of the morning completely shattered. A small crowd had gathered, people clustering near Vince's shop, their necks craned as they tried to peer past the police tape stretched across the doorframe.

The tape fluttered in the ocean breeze and an officer stood guard near the entrance, firm but bored, while others moved in and out of the building as they processed the scene.

"Looks like the circus came to town," Lois muttered, her voice low but tinged with irritation.

I didn't answer, too busy staring at the tape and the uniformed officers. My place—my bakery—was now part of a crime scene. My stomach churned, and I had to resist the urge to get closer and see if anything new was happening.

The crowd murmured with a mix of excitement and unease, snippets of conversation floating through the salty air.

"I heard it was a robbery," one woman whispered to her companion, clutching her oversized tote bag like a lifeline.

"No, no—someone said that Rinaldi boy finally got himself

in trouble," the man next to her replied, his voice smug, as if he'd been expecting it.

"Who's the body, then?" a younger man asked, leaning against the boardwalk railing as we all watched paramedics removing the body on a stretcher.

Lois gave a small huff beside me, clearly unimpressed with the growing game of telephone.

"This town sure knows how to keep itself entertained," she muttered, but then her eyes caught on something—or rather, someone. A woman was pushing her way through the crowd, her movements frantic and her sobs audible even above the low hum of voices.

"Lois!" the woman called out, her voice breaking as she stumbled toward us.

The woman looked to be in her early thirties, with a blotchy, tear-streaked face and hair that had been pulled into a ponytail in a rush. Her sweatshirt hung unevenly over her shoulders, one sleeve pushed up, the other drooping. She looked like someone barely holding it together.

"Lois!" she cried again, rushing forward and gripping Lois's arm like a lifeline. "I heard you were there. I heard you found him—found Marcus."

Lois stiffened slightly at the contact, but didn't pull away. "Beth," she said gently, her tone cautious. "I'm so sorry. This is... awful. I can't imagine how you're feeling."

"I can't believe it," Beth sobbed, her voice cracking as she stumbled over her words. "He just got back to town, and now—now he's gone! It doesn't feel real."

I stayed a few steps behind, unsure of whether to step in or stay out of the way. My heart ached for Beth, even though I didn't know her. Her grief was raw, and it filled the air like a heavy, suffocating fog.

Beth's sobs quieted slightly as Lois gently steered her a step away from the crowd, giving them a bit of space. I followed cautiously, staying close enough to hear but not wanting to intrude.

"He came to see me last night, Lois," Beth said, her voice trembling. She swiped at her cheeks with the back of her hand, taking a deep, shaky breath. "After all these years... he just showed up. Out of the blue."

Lois's eyebrows lifted in surprise. "Last night? What did he want?"

Beth hesitated, glancing around as if unsure whether to continue. "I—I told him about our son," she finally said, her voice breaking again. "He didn't even know. I thought... I thought he deserved to know. And I thought maybe he'd... he'd want to meet him."

"And did he?" Lois asked, her tone cautious but kind.

Beth shook her head, her tears starting up again. "No. He got upset. I don't know if it was shock or guilt or what, but he barely said a word. Just kept pacing, like he was trying to figure out what to do." She sniffed, her shoulders slumping. "And then he left. Just walked out the door."

Lois frowned, clearly trying to process the information. "Did he say where he was going?"

Beth nodded slowly. "He mentioned... he said there was something he needed to do, but he didn't explain. And then this morning, I heard..." Her voice cracked, and she covered her face with her hands, her shoulders shaking with fresh sobs.

My stomach twisted as I listened, my lawyer mind kicking in and processing what Beth was saying. From what I'd heard, Marcus had been gone for years. Why come back now? And what had he needed to do so urgently? And it sounded like he and Beth had a child together. I hated feeling so out of the loop when everyone else seemed to know everything. Hazards of being new in town, I supposed.

Lois awkwardly patted Beth's shoulder, her face a mix of sympathy and unease. "I'm so sorry, Beth. I really am."

Beth sniffled and glanced up at Lois. "I don't know what to do. I thought—I thought maybe there'd be a chance for him to know his son, and now..." she trailed off, shaking her head.

Lois gave her a reassuring squeeze. "You don't have to figure it all out right now. Just take care of yourself, okay? And your boy. You've got people here who care about you."

Beth nodded, though her eyes were glassy and distant. "At least it's all over now."

I wondered what was over, the relationship? The hopes of having a father for her son? But before the conversation went any further, she gave Lois a quick half smile and then walked away down the boardwalk toward town, her sobs quieter now but still audible. Lois watched her go for a moment before turning to me, her shoulders slumping.

"Beth Mitchell and Marcus go way back," Lois explained, her voice low. "They were high school sweethearts. Everyone in town knew about them. Then Beth got pregnant right before graduation."

"And he left?" I asked, piecing the timeline together.

Lois nodded grimly. "He skipped town right around the same time. I know Beth never told him about the baby. Word was he went to stay with some relatives up north, but no one's seen or heard from him since. Beth's had a rough go of it, raising her son on her own. She's done alright, though. Got a good job, good kid." She paused, shaking her head. "And now this, right after she finally tells him about his son? Life sure can be cruel."

I nodded slowly, filing away the information as the murmurs of the crowd filled the air around us.

Lois sighed and crossed her arms, glancing back at the police tape stretched across Vince's shop. "Well, this morning sure got complicated in a hurry." She huffed out a breath as she took it all in. "Small-town life teaches you to roll with the punches. But this..." Her gaze lingered on the shop. "This feels like it's gonna stick around for a while."

I followed her eyes, feeling the weight of the morning settle in my chest. I hadn't been here long, but it was clear that Marcus's death was going to leave a ripple in Moonstone Bay—a ripple I might already be caught in.

Lois gave me a nudge on the arm. "Alright, let's get out of here before someone decides we're worth questioning again. You good to head back?"

"Yeah," I replied, though my thoughts were still swirling.

As we turned to leave, I cast one last glance at the police tape, the weight of the unanswered questions pressing heavy on my mind. Marcus Holloway had come back to town after decades away, only to meet this violent end. Whatever secrets he'd been carrying, they weren't buried with him—not yet.

8

I went back to my bungalow and plopped down on the couch, completely drained. The morning had been nothing short of surreal, and my thoughts churned as I stared at the ceiling.

Shortcake hopped up beside me and settled in, purring, before I even touched him. I scratched behind his ears, grateful for the soothing rhythm of his contentment.

"What a day, buddy." Anxiety crept in. What did all this mean for my fledgling business? How long would the police take to process the scene? And what about Vince? Could he have killed someone?

My stomach knotted at the thought of Vince in handcuffs, but I couldn't stop the pang of concern. It wasn't just about the business—it was Vince himself. I barely knew him, but something about him had gotten under my skin. I realized that I very much hoped he hadn't killed someone, and not just because it would create chaos around my bakery idea. I wanted him to be innocent because I was interested in him in a romantic way. It was a shock to realize it, but I couldn't deny the way my heart flip-flopped every time I saw him, the way he'd made me feel that very first time our eyes had met. I had it bad for the guy, and even seeing him in the state he was in this morning didn't put a damper on those feelings. It made me sad for him. He clearly had some issues. But it didn't make me any less infatuated.

Which was absolutely crazy. I'd just met the man barely twenty-four hours before and I'd only recently gotten out of a bad marriage. After things had fallen apart with Christopher, I'd vowed to have nothing to do with men for a very long time. A very long time wasn't three months.

But my heart said otherwise.

"This is insane," I told Shortcake, running a hand over my face. "What am I even doing here?" Shortcake blinked up at me, unimpressed by my existential crisis.

I needed a distraction, something to get me out of my head.

I pushed off the couch and headed into the kitchen, where my grandmother's recipe book sat on the counter, still untouched from the night before. I flipped through the worn pages absentmindedly, looking for something that felt doable until I landed on a simple yeast bread recipe I remembered making for Christopher once. It wasn't a fancy recipe, but it was reliable—a perfect way to clear my mind. I wanted to test it too, because I had a feeling it was going to end up being a staple for the bakery.

As I measured flour and water and mixed the dough, I thought more about the bakery. I'd planned to sell bread along with pastries, pies, and other sweets, but the logistics of making enough loaves to keep up with demand felt daunting suddenly. Making one loaf was all well and good, but enough to run a bakery? That was going to be a new challenge.

"How do bakeries even do this?" I wondered aloud, creating a mental list of things to research: commercial ovens, proofing techniques, finding bulk ingredients. The deeper I thought about it, the more out of my depth I felt.

Still, as I kneaded the dough, some of my tension eased. Baking had always been my way of finding balance. No matter how uncertain life seemed, there was something comforting about the simplicity of flour, water, and yeast coming together into something nourishing.

I also found some comfort in the fact that Moonstone Bay was currently in the off season. I would have months to work things out before the summer crowd came.

I'd just set the dough aside to rise when there was a knock at the door. Wiping my hands on a dish towel, I opened it to find Sheriff Donovan standing on the porch.

He was older than I'd realized before, a dusting of grey sparkling in the sunshine and deep lines etching his face. His expression was serious, but his tone was polite as he said, "Sorry to bother you, Ms. Malone. Just wanted to follow up about what happened this morning."

I stepped aside, gesturing for him to come in. "Of course. Can I offer you some coffee?"

"No, thanks," he replied, taking a seat at my small kitchen table. Shortcake leapt onto the back of the couch, watching Donovan with narrowed eyes.

"Your cat doesn't seem thrilled about my visit," Donovan said with a faint smile.

I gave Shortcake a look. "Don't mind him. He thinks he runs the place."

Donovan pulled out a small notebook and clicked his pen. "Let's go back to what you saw this morning. Can you remember any more details?"

I recounted the events step by step, from seeing the broken glass to entering the shop and finding the body. I tried to keep my description as clear and precise as possible, though my

stomach tightened as I remembered the metallic smell in the air
and the eerie stillness of Marcus's figure on the floor.

Donovan nodded occasionally, jotting down notes but
keeping his expression neutral. When I finished, he looked up.
"Thanks. That's helpful."

He paused, then tilted his head slightly. "What brings you
to Moonstone Bay, Ms. Malone? You're not a local."

"No," I said, shaking my head. "I'm from San Francisco. I
moved here a few days ago to... start fresh, I guess."

He raised an eyebrow, and I added, "I'm an attorney. Criminal defense, mostly. But I'm on a break from that now."

His expression shifted slightly, a flicker of respect passing
over his face before his professional mask returned. "A criminal
attorney? I suppose you've seen your fair share of situations like
this, then."

"More than I'd like to admit," I replied, feeling the familiar
tug of courtroom memories.

Donovan set his pen down and regarded me for a moment.
"Let me guess—you're already building a defense for Rinaldi in
your head."

I stiffened slightly, caught off guard by his tone. "I'm just
saying it's worth keeping an open mind. Why would Vince—
assuming he's guilty—shoot someone and then fall asleep right
next to the gun? It doesn't add up."

Donovan leaned back slightly, his brows knitting together
as he considered my question. "Maybe he panicked. Maybe he
was drunk. There are a dozen ways it could've happened."

I shook my head, seeing Shorty shift on the couch behind
Donovan. His ears flicked, as if he were following every word.
"It still doesn't make sense. Falling asleep next to the evidence
is practically begging to be caught. Vince might not be polished,
but I doubt he's that careless."

Donovan's eyes narrowed, though his tone remained calm.

"And you don't think your judgment might be... clouded? No disrespect, but you're new here. And you two have a business relationship. You've only been in town a couple of days, and I'd bet you don't know Vince as well as you think you do."

I opened my mouth to argue, but Shorty let out a loud meow, startling both of us. Donovan glanced over his shoulder at the cat, who flicked his tail, clearly unimpressed by the tension.

"He's opinionated," I said lightly, hoping to ease the moment.

Donovan turned back to me, the corners of his mouth quirking up slightly. "Seems like he's not the only one."

"I'm just pointing out that this doesn't feel straightforward," I said, folding my arms. "And you don't strike me as the kind of sheriff who jumps to conclusions."

His faint smile faded, replaced by a more guarded expression. "And you don't strike me as the kind of attorney who avoids playing devil's advocate."

I couldn't help a small smile of my own, despite the tension. "Fair enough."

Donovan stood, slipping his notebook into his pocket. "Thanks for your time, Ms. Malone. If you think of anything else, give me a call. We're finished over at the office space, so you're welcome to get back to work." He glanced at the bowl of rising dough on the counter. "Good luck with the bakery—and stay out of trouble."

I walked him to the door, holding it open as he stepped out onto the porch. Shortcake followed me, his tail flicking as he glared after Donovan.

"What am I doing, Shorty?" I muttered, closing the door and leaning against it. My gaze shifted to the ramshackle place I now called home. "This is not how starting over was supposed to go."

9

After Sheriff Donovan left, I heated the oven for the bread and then grabbed my cleaning supplies. The bungalow was charming in its own neglected, cobwebby way, but before I could start dreaming about renovations on the little place, I needed to see it under all the dust and grime.

I tied a bandana over my curls and slipped on a pair of rubber gloves, armed with a spray bottle in one hand and a rag in the other. Shortcake perched on the windowsill, his tail flicking as he watched me wage war against decades of dirt.

"Laugh it up, Shorty," I muttered, scrubbing at the kitchen cabinets as the cat went about aggressively cleaning his paws. The dingy white paint was peeling in places, revealing patches of solid pine wood beneath. I'd need to repaint eventually, or strip the paint and leave it all natural. But for now, I just wanted to make the place feel livable.

Cobwebs came down in thick clumps as I wiped along the edges of the ceiling, and the baseboards practically sighed with relief as the rag passed over them. I stuck the bread in the oven when it came to temperature and the faint smell of baking bread began to weave its way through the bungalow, warm and inviting, chasing away the stale, musty odor that had clung to the place since I'd arrived.

I lost myself in cleaning and was surprised a while later when the oven timer dinged. Thankfully, I'd just finished with the deep clean of the kitchen and I tossed my gloves into the sink, ready for a break. "Progress," I said, wiping my forehead. It wasn't much, but it was a start.

The warm aroma of yeast and flour filled the air as I pulled the golden loaf from the oven and set it on the cooling rack. The crust was a deep, even brown, and as I tapped the bottom lightly, the hollow sound reassured me that it had baked perfectly.

There was something so satisfying about baking, the way a handful of simple ingredients—flour, water, yeast—could transform into something as solid and comforting as bread. My grandmother always said baking was part alchemy, part therapy, and I believed it now as I stared at the beautiful loaf I'd created.

I closed my eyes and inhaled deeply, letting the scent wrap around me. It was a warm, cozy smell, the kind that could make even the most uncertain day feel just a little more manageable. The kitchen felt brighter, lighter, despite the events of the morning.

But as I leaned against the counter, staring at the loaf, the weight of the day crept back in. Marcus Holloway. Vince in handcuffs. The sheriff's questions. It all replayed in my mind like a film I couldn't shut off.

Sheriff Donovan's visit had been cordial enough, but the tension between us lingered. I could tell he was sizing me up, trying to decide if I was just a nosy newcomer or someone worth keeping an eye on. The way he'd mentioned Vince—almost dismissively—bothered me. I wasn't sure what I believed yet, but my gut said Vince wasn't capable of cold-blooded murder and I hoped the sheriff felt that way, too.

Shortcake jumped down from the windowsill and trotted into the kitchen, his tail high as he leapt onto the counter and sniffed toward the bread. His green eyes darted up to meet mine, wide with feigned innocence.

"Don't even think about it," I said, wagging a finger at him.

He blinked slowly, his tail flicking as he reached out a single paw and tapped the edge of the cooling rack, testing his limits.

"Oh, alright," I muttered, tearing off a small corner of the crust and holding it out. "Just a nibble."

He leaned forward, his nose twitching, before he snatched the piece from my fingers. I watched him chew, smug satisfaction all over his face.

"See? You're already eating into my profits," I teased, scratching behind his ears.

I watched him gnaw at the crust and although I knew better than to slice into bread straight out of the oven, I grabbed a knife and dug in. It was too delicious to resist, the crust chewy and golden and the inside light and fluffy. Just about right, although I could imagine it even better with a little rosemary and some garlic cloves. Maybe I could offer multiple options at the bakery.

I grabbed my notebook from the counter and sat at the small kitchen table, the rest of the loaf cooling behind me. Flipping to a blank page, I wrote "Bakery To-Do List" across the top, underlining it twice for good measure.

The words looked neat and full of promise, but my thoughts were anything but organized. Suppliers, ovens, proofing racks—it was a mountain of logistics I wasn't sure how to climb. I scribbled down a few vague ideas, but each new item seemed to raise more questions than answers. I would definitely need to do some internet research later, start chipping away at all the things I didn't know about running a bakery.

Shortcake hopped down from the counter and sat beside my chair, his wide green eyes fixed on me like he could sense my unease.

"What do you think, Shortcake?" I asked, leaning down to scratch his chin. "Too late to back out now, huh?"

He purred softly, his tail curling around his paws, and I let out a small laugh. "Yeah, that's what I thought."

For a moment, the smell of bread and the rhythmic scratching of my pen helped to quiet the anxiety in my mind. But the calm didn't last long. My phone rang suddenly, slicing through the moment like a knife.

I glanced at the screen, my stomach lurching when I saw the words "Moonstone Bay Jail."

My hand hovered over the phone as I hesitated. Finally, I picked it up.

"Hello?"

A familiar voice came through, tired but steady. "Hey, Ginny. It's Vince."

I straightened, startled to hear his voice. "Vince? How are you calling me right now?"

"Jail phones, fancy stuff," he replied with a dry chuckle, though it lacked any real humor. "Turns out, I can still make calls. That's about the only perk of my situation."

My grip on the phone tightened. "I take it things aren't going well."

"No, not really," he admitted, his voice heavy with exhaustion. "The sheriff's pretty sure I did it, and I can't exactly afford to sit in here while they sort this out. Which is why I'm calling you."

I frowned, unease pooling in my stomach. "Okay... what's going on?"

He hesitated for a beat, then sighed. "I've got to sell the office space to make bail."

"What?" My voice rose before I could stop it.

"There's a guy here in town who's wanted to buy the place for a while, and I just called him up. He's more than happy to take it off my hands. I'm really sorry. I know you were excited about the bakery."

I felt like the floor had fallen out beneath me. My stomach dropped, and I was amazed to realize just how much I had invested in this crazy dream of mine in such a short amount of time.

Pacing, I tried to figure out another way. "Isn't there someone who could loan you the money for a while? Could you sell your car, maybe?"

He laughed. "My car is maybe worth a thousand dollars. Wouldn't help even if I did. And then what would I do with myself?" He sighed on the other end. "Look, I'm really on the tail end of broke. I hate to admit it but those are the facts. I'm a loser with a failing business, a beater car, and the office space. If I want to get out of jail, the office space is gonna have to go. And believe me, I want to get out of jail. If I can figure out who murdered Marcus Holloway, it might save me from jail and save my business. People hire P.I.s who solve murders."

I bit my lip and looked up at the ceiling. I could hear my mother shriek as the next words came out of my mouth. "What if *I* gave you the money for bail?"

There was silence on the other end, and I was sure he thought I was absolutely bonkers. *I* thought I was absolutely bonkers, too. But I wanted that bakery and I wanted it bad. I didn't want to wait. I didn't want to negotiate a new lease somewhere else. The crazy thing was, I wanted the bakery in that shop and with Vince running a private investigation business in the back. The thought of it tickled me so much that I was willing to make this big bet and help him get out of jail.

In the back of my mind, though, there was still a question. Did he really kill that man?

I shoved it away, deciding that the best way for me to answer that question was to be around Vince and observe. Turn all those expensive lawyerly skills in his direction and try to make sense of it all in a logical way. Half a dozen years as a criminal attorney gave me a pretty good instinct about criminals, and I intended to use that instinct to decide for myself whether Vince was innocent or not.

"Are you serious?" he asked quietly.

"I'm serious."

"Wow, okay! Thank you! I can't believe you'd do this for me. I know I haven't exactly given you the best impression in the couple of times we met, but I promise I'm not what you think..."

"Don't worry about it," I said with a laugh as I flew around the bungalow looking for my shoes and purse. "Alright, I'll be over there soon."

I couldn't believe what I was doing. It felt crazy and reckless. But I'd spent the first thirty-four years of life being sane and careful and look where that had gotten me. Once again, I was leaning into this gut thing. Yeah, it was crazy and reckless. But also, it felt really good.

10

After a couple of hours wrangling with a bail bondsman and navigating the endless paperwork, I finally managed to get Vince out of jail. We were mostly quiet on the short ride from the police department back to the boardwalk, each of us lost in our own thoughts.

Now, as we approached the shop, the golden light of early evening stretched long shadows across the boardwalk. The breeze carried a faint scent of salt, mingling with the rich smell of fried seafood from the diner. Laughter and the occasional clink of glass drifted toward us, a reminder that, for the rest of the town, it was just another night.

Vince walked beside me, his hands stuffed into his pockets, his head slightly bowed. His easygoing swagger was absent, replaced by a heaviness that hung around him like a storm cloud.

"Thanks again," he said suddenly, his voice low and gruff. "For getting me out of there. I—I didn't mean for any of this to mess up your plans."

I glanced over at him, surprised by the apology. "It's not

your fault. And I'm sure the police think that too, even if it doesn't seem like it. I'm sure they were just doing their job."

He snorted softly. "Yeah, well, their 'job' includes pinning this on me because I happened to be in the wrong place at the wrong time." He paused, his brow furrowing. "I swear, Ginny, I didn't kill Marcus. I couldn't—"

"I believe you," I said quickly, cutting him off. The words came out more firmly than I expected, but they were true. I didn't know Vince well, but something in my gut told me he wasn't capable of what they were accusing him of.

His shoulders relaxed a little, and he nodded. "Thanks," he murmured.

When we got closer to the shop, a man pacing out front caught my attention. His sharp movements stood out against the calm of the boardwalk, his wiry frame silhouetted against the vibrant orange of the sky. He was dressed in business casual —an expensive jacket and slacks—but the ensemble looked out of place in Moonstone Bay's laid-back atmosphere. His hands were shoved into his pockets, and when he saw us, his face twisted into a sneer.

"Rinaldi," he barked, striding toward us. "I thought you agreed to sell the place to me! Why are you stringing me along?"

Vince stiffened immediately, his posture shifting. He reached out and gently pulled me behind him, his stance protective as he faced the man. I blinked at the sudden move-ment, startled but not entirely unhappy about it.

"Things have changed," Vince said evenly, though I could hear the edge creeping into his voice. He glanced over his shoulder at me, offering a faint, awkward smile that made my stomach flip. "I found a guardian angel."

The man—who I guessed must be the infamous buyer— shot me a withering look. "Look, I'm willing to pay you ten thousand over what I offered earlier," he said, trailing behind us as we approached the door of the shop. "You need the money, Rinaldi. Look at you."

Vince's head snapped up from the door where he'd been fumbling with his keys. His eyes were angry and there was a steely set to his jaw. I liked what I saw there, all raw power and rage. This man could be a force to be reckoned with, if he could just get out of his own way.

"Get out of here, Parker," Vince said, his voice low and cold. "I'm not selling."

The man sneered at Vince, then at me. His eyes lingered a beat too long, making my skin crawl. "You're making a mistake, Rinaldi. You'll come crawling back when you're desperate. I know your type."

Vince closed the door in his face and locked it, although the big front pane was still broken so I wasn't sure how much good the lock was going to do. Although I was happy to see that the door actually did lock properly and wasn't broken after all. Small blessings.

The air inside the shop was stuffy and carried the faint metallic tang of the morning's events.

"Sorry about that. Wyatt Parker's been trying to get this place from me for years and he thought he'd finally got me when I called him earlier for the bail money." He kicked at the empty vodka bottle, then picked it up and threw it in a trashcan in the corner. Then his eyes lit up, and he met my gaze with a smile. "But then I got the satisfaction of calling him back and telling him never mind. Talk about satisfying."

He leaned against the edge of his desk, a small, smug smile playing at his lips. "We've hated each other since high school. It's a long story."

"Sounds like there's a lot of history between you two," I said, crossing my arms as I leaned back against the counter.

Vince nodded, the humor slipping from his face. "Yeah. But it's not just him. This place means something to me. It was my parents' before it was mine. They opened their insurance business here when I was a kid. I guess I've been trying to hold on to it ever since they died. Feels like the last piece of them I have left."

The confession hit me harder than I expected. I suddenly saw Vince not as the messy P.I. who'd passed out drunk in his office, but as someone carrying the weight of loss, clinging to this place not just as a business but as a tether to his past.

"I get it," I said softly. "And for what it's worth, I think you made the right call, not selling the place."

"I didn't kill him, Ginny," he said as he ran a hand through that thick, dark hair. He met my gaze and electricity passed between us. We both stared at each other for longer than was necessary, which is how I knew he felt it too. Our bodies angled subtly closer. I wanted him to reach out, to kiss me, to pull me into him. I wanted to feel his touch.

He reached out and brushed my arm very lightly. "You believe me, right? I never would have killed someone. My whole job is trying to bring justice and closure to the people of Moonstone Bay. At least when they hire me to do it."

His touch sent a spark all through me.

I nodded, my heart hammering in my chest. "I do," I said quietly. And it wasn't just hormones talking. I couldn't reconcile the Vince I'd seen today—the one with raw emotion in his voice and an almost desperate need to clear his name—with the image of a cold-blooded killer.

Besides, the pieces didn't fit. If Vince had killed Marcus, why would he leave the gun out and fall asleep next to it? It made no sense.

Then, as if realizing the moment had stretched too long, he

stepped back, running a hand over the back of his neck. "I appreciate you bailing me out, Ginny. More than I can say."

"Don't mention it," I said with a shaky laugh, trying to ignore the lingering warmth where his hand had touched my arm.

"It's Valentine's Day," I said suddenly, the realization slamming into me and tumbling out before I could stop it.

Vince snorted, shaking his head. "Yeah, it is. Worst day of the year, if you ask me."

I laughed softly. "You won't get an argument from me. I forgot all about it until just now."

"Lucky you," he said dryly. "I didn't forget, but not because I wanted to remember. Valentine's Day... it wasn't exactly my strong suit. My ex-wife made that pretty clear every year we were married."

I tilted my head, intrigued. "Lois mentioned you were divorced."

He nodded, his gaze distant for a moment. "Yeah. Cara wanted more than what I could give her. More romance, more excitement, more... everything. And honestly? She wasn't wrong. I'm not the hearts-and-flowers type, and being a P.I. in a small town isn't exactly glamorous."

The self-deprecation in his voice made me ache for him, but I kept my tone light. "Well, you're in good company. This is my first Valentine's Day post-divorce, and I can't say I'm sorry to be spending it like this instead of at some overpriced prix fixe dinner."

That earned me a small smile, and for a moment, the tension between us eased.

"What happened with your ex, if you don't mind me asking?" he asked.

I shrugged. "We just weren't a good fit. He wanted me to be someone I wasn't, and I guess I wanted the same from him.

Eventually, we both realized it wasn't going to work, so we called it quits."

"Clean break?" he asked, his tone curious but not prying.

"More or less," I said, not wanting to get into the messier details. "We both walked away with what we needed, and I ended up here, so I guess it all worked out."

"Lucky us," he said with a wry grin, the faintest hint of humor creeping back into his expression.

I leaned against the bare wall, glancing around the shop as the conversation shifted to easier topics. "Lois is going to get started on the renovations soon. She said it shouldn't take long to get the place up to code and set up for the bakery. I'll see if she can get over here in the morning to fix that front window."

"That's good," Vince said, straightening a little. "You won't have to worry about me getting in the way. It's not like I've got a packed schedule. And with all the talk about the murder, I don't think my phone's going to be ringing off the hook with business anytime soon."

"Maybe that'll change," I said, trying to sound hopeful. "If you figure out what really happened to Marcus, it could turn things around for you. People love a good redemption story."

He chuckled softly, though it didn't quite reach his eyes. "Yeah, we'll see."

We fell into a comfortable silence for a moment, the weight of the day settling around us. I glanced over at Vince, watching as he absentmindedly rubbed the back of his neck. There was something about him that drew me in—his quiet strength, his vulnerability, the way he seemed to carry the weight of the world, but still managed a crooked smile.

He lingered for a moment longer, his gaze meeting mine like he wanted to say something else but thought better of it. Then he straightened and nodded toward the door. "I should let you get going. It's been a long day."

"It has," I agreed, though I wasn't entirely ready to leave.

As Vince walked me to the door, I couldn't help but steal one last glance at him. Despite the messy circumstances that had brought us together, I felt a strange sense of optimism. Maybe this move wasn't so crazy after all.

"Good night, Vince," I said, stepping outside into the cool evening air.

"Good night, Ginny."

As I walked away, I caught myself smiling, though a sliver of doubt crept into my thoughts. I hoped I wasn't wrong about him—about his innocence, his intentions, and everything in between.

"Please don't let me be wrong about him," I whispered to myself, the words lost in the salty breeze.

11

The next day, I got up bright and early, ready to make progress on the bungalow and the bakery plans. I started baking early, wanting to test out as many recipes from my grandmother's recipe book as possible before I opened the shop doors. I knew it would take me years to go through every recipe, but I wanted to unearth as many gems as possible to get things off the ground with a bang.

The tangy smell of yeast filled the air as I leaned over the counter, kneading dough with as steady a hand as I could muster. Today I was working on a chocolate pecan loaf. I would turn into big boules of slightly sweet bread. Flour dusted every available surface, including my shirt, which was starting to look more white than blue.

"You think I should try a cinnamon swirl loaf next?" I asked Shortcake, who was perched on the far end of the counter. His green eyes locked on me. He flicked his tail, unimpressed, and reached out a paw to slap at a canister of cocoa powder sitting nearby.

"Don't you dare," I warned, narrowing my eyes at him.

He froze, staring at me with what I could only describe as

pure defiance. Then, with one swift motion, the cocoa toppled onto the floor. The lid popped off, sending a cloud of brown dust into the air.

"Shorty!" I groaned, waving the air clear. He jumped down from the counter and strutted through the mess like a king, leaving a trail of powdery paw prints behind him.

"You're mad because I haven't taken you to the shop yet, aren't you?" I muttered, grabbing a damp rag. "I can feel it. This is your little rebellion."

Shortcake meowed loudly from the floor, pawing at the mess like he was proud of his work.

As I bent down to clean, my phone buzzed on the counter. I glanced at the screen, spotting "Mom" in big, bold letters. My first instinct was to ignore it—again. But I'd already avoided two of her calls since finding the body the day before, and I knew she'd only get more persistent if I didn't answer.

Sighing, I grabbed the phone and pressed it to my ear. "Hi, Mom."

"Virginia!" Her voice came through loud and clear, brimming with that specific mix of concern and criticism only she could manage. "I was beginning to think you'd fallen off the face of the earth. What are you doing out there? I've been worried!"

"I'm fine, Mom," I said, keeping my tone light. "Just busy, that's all."

"Busy with what? You're not working, are you? You told me you were taking time off."

"I *am* taking time off," I assured her, wiping cocoa from the counter with one hand. "I've just been... settling in."

She made a disapproving noise, the kind that made me feel like I was sixteen again. "Settling in? How long is this little escape supposed to last, anyway? Surely you're not planning to stay out there forever."

I bit my lip, swallowing the urge to snap back. "I don't know, Mom. I'm just taking it one day at a time."

"Well, I hope you're not wasting your education. You worked so hard to get where you were. You can't just throw that all away to play house in some tiny beach town."

I closed my eyes, taking a deep breath. "I'm not throwing anything away, Mom. I'm just... figuring things out."

There was a pause, long enough to make me wonder if she was choosing her words carefully. "Maybe I should come visit. I could help you sort through things. Get on with your life a little quicker."

"No!" The word came out too fast, too loud. I cleared my throat, softening my tone. "I mean, not right now. The place is kind of a mess, and I don't have anywhere for you to stay."

"Virginia, what are you up to?" she asked, her tone shifting to suspicion.

"Nothing nefarious," I said with a weak laugh. "Just trying to get my head straight. I promise I'll call you soon."

"You'd better," she said, her voice tinged with worry. "I love you, sweetheart."

"Love you too, Mom," I replied, ending the call before she could dig any deeper.

After cleaning up the cocoa and giving Shortcake a pointed glare, I poured myself a cup of tea and stepped out onto the small front porch. The bungalow's wild overgrown garden stretched out before me, full of tangled vines and rogue flowers blooming in defiance of any order.

I sank into the old creaky rocking chair and sipped my tea, letting the salty breeze wash over me. It felt like another world compared to my old life, where every minute was scheduled, every detail meticulously planned.

How long had I been here? A few days? A week? It wasn't long, but already I felt like a different person. Like this little beach town was peeling away layers of the old me, revealing someone I hadn't met yet. The thought was incredibly exciting to me and I smiled.

Shortcake appeared at my feet a minute later, tail twitching as he hopped onto the porch railing. I reached out to scratch his head, my thoughts drifting to Fran's words at the diner.

"You don't think it has anything to do with Alma, do you?"

The name had hung in the air like a ghost in the diner the day before. Fran's reaction had been cautious, almost fearful, and Lois hadn't offered much in the way of answers.

I glanced back inside, where my phone sat on the counter. The thought of diving into old news articles tugged at me, but I hesitated. Did I really want to go down that rabbit hole? Maybe I would be better off staying out of it all, focusing on the business I was trying to get off the ground.

Shortcake nudged my hand, drawing me out of my thoughts. "What do you think, Shorty?" I asked, half-laughing. "Should I dig around a little? See what I can find?"

He flicked his tail, as if saying *it couldn't do any harm to look.*

The idea wouldn't let go, so after setting my tea down, I went inside and grabbed my phone. Back on the porch, I opened the search bar and typed "Alma Moonstone Bay." A few results popped up, and I clicked on the first article, scanning the text quickly.

"High School Senior Missing, Foul Play Suspected."

The headline alone made my stomach twist. Alma Ramirez, a Moonstone Bay High senior, had disappeared just weeks before her graduation nearly twenty years ago. The article described her as a bright, driven young woman with plenty of prospects as one of the top students in her class. She'd been last seen near the boardwalk late at night, and though police had investigated, no body or evidence had ever been found.

I stared at the grainy photo of Alma, taken from her yearbook. Her almond-shaped eyes sparkled with quiet confidence, her smile unguarded and full of hope.

"What happened to you, Alma?" I murmured, scrolling down for more information.

But there wasn't much else. No follow-ups, no break-throughs, just a vague mention that the case had gone cold within months. Rumors swirled in the comments section of the archived article: some believed Alma had run away, while others were convinced something darker had happened.

Fran's warning echoed in my mind. "Nothing good comes from sticking your nose in someone else's mess."

I put the phone down, staring out at the garden as the breeze rustled through the wildflowers. Fran had warned us to stay out of it, but now I couldn't help but wonder if Alma's disappearance and Marcus's death were connected. Why else would Fran have mentioned it as we talked about Marcus' death? Was this more than a coincidence?

Shortcake hopped onto the chair with me, curling up on my lap, his tail curling around my wrist. I scratched behind his ears absentmindedly, my mind spinning with possibilities. I wondered who else might be able to tell me more about the girl who'd disappeared and the man who'd just been murdered.

"Might be time to visit the local library," I said quietly as I pet Shorty's head, though I wasn't sure if I was ready for the answers I might find.

Still, I wanted to know what was going on. I wanted to know why Marcus had been killed where I was about to open a bakery, and if there was anything else I didn't know about, that might become a problem.

12

A couple of hours later, the smell of chocolate pecan bread filled the bungalow as I slid the loaf out of the oven, its golden crust crackling faintly as it hit the cooling rack. I leaned against the counter, breathing in the aroma and congratulating myself on a job well done.

I'd spent most of the morning sifting through recipes and working on the bungalow. The place was now more or less clean, but there was plenty of work to do. I found leaky faucets, peeling paint, water damaged walls, and more. But nothing that I couldn't tackle. At least I didn't think so. The heater was still not working, and I'd burned through nearly all of my wood. Added to the flour I'd baked through, I would need to make another trip to the store before too long.

The doorbell rang as I stood in the kitchen making a grocery list. It gave out a sickly, off-pitch jingle that made me laugh out loud. "Shorty, did you hear that?" I called out, grabbing a towel to wipe my hands. "Sounds like someone stepped on a squeaky toy."

Shortcake didn't respond—he was busy sprawled on the

windowsill, twitching his tail, pretending not to care about visitors.

When I opened the door, Lois stood on the porch with a massive white dog by her side. The animal looked like a walking cloud, its thick fur practically glowing in the late afternoon sun.

"Hey there!" Lois greeted, her grin as wide as her dog was fluffy. "Hope you don't mind—Princess insisted on coming. She doesn't really do alone time. But I can leave her out here on the porch if you don't want her inside. She does shed like a maniac. I'm not gonna lie."

I laughed. "No worries on shedding, we've got enough of our own fur to make a coat out of, right, Shortcake?" I called to the cat, who'd disappeared into my bedroom. "Wow, she's beautiful," I said, stepping back to let them in. "Does she get along with cats?"

Lois waved a hand dismissively. "Oh, Princess loves everybody. She's basically a four-legged goodwill ambassador."

The giant dog wagged her tail slowly as she trotted into the bungalow, her nails clicking softly against the floor.

A minute later, Shortcake sauntered back into the room with an irritated meow. He froze when he spotted Princess, his tail puffing up slightly as he assessed the situation.

Princess, for her part, sat down and thumped her tail against the floor, radiating pure canine friendliness. She tilted her head, her tongue lolling out as if to say, *What's your problem, tiny guy?*

Shorty took a tentative step closer, his nose twitching. After a moment of mutual sniffing, he flicked his tail in what I could only interpret as reluctant approval.

"They're gonna be best friends, I can tell," Lois said with a laugh.

"Or mortal enemies," I countered, watching as Shortcake

circled Princess once before hopping onto the couch and curling up on a cushion. To my surprise, Princess followed suit, hauling her massive frame onto the opposite end of the couch with a sigh.

"Princess! Off," Lois barked, but the dog ignored her completely.

"It's fine," I said, waving her off. "The couch is ancient, anyway. She can have it."

"You sure?" Lois asked, though her tone suggested she knew she'd already lost the battle.

I shrugged. "She looks more comfortable there than I've ever been."

Shortcake stretched out along the couch's backrest, inching closer to Princess like he was staking a claim. Within minutes, they were nestled together like old friends.

"You want to try my chocolate pecan bread?" I asked, gesturing toward the counter as we turned away from the animals. "Fresh out of the oven."

"Wow, absolutely! It smells delicious," Lois said, her eyes lighting up.

I cut her a thick slice of the chocolate pecan loaf, and she took a bite, her expression shifting to pure bliss. "Holy cow. You could open a bakery tomorrow with stuff like this."

"Good to know," I said with a smile. "Hopefully by next month I'll be close to that."

Lois pulled a roll of sketches from under her arm and spread them across the small kitchen table. "Well, that's good because I got the permits approved this morning."

My eyebrows shot up. "Already? That's fast."

"What can I say?" Lois said with a wink. "I've got connections. I showed them plans I worked up, although of course, I'll need your final approval and need to file any updates with the city. I'm guessing you'll want to change a few things, but I couldn't stop myself. I thought it would be best if we got our plans in with them early."

I laughed. "Good thinking. I'm happy you're ready to make this thing happen. I am too."

She sat down across from me as she pointed to her sketches and started to walk me through her plans. "Alright, here's what I'm thinking. We'll start by tearing into this wall to plumb for a sink, then we'll add the ovens over here. What's your capacity goal? Two ovens? Three?"

"Let's go with three," I said after a moment of thought. "Better to have too much space than not enough."

"Smart," Lois said, scribbling something in her notebook. "I'll make sure it's all up to code and ready to handle commercial baking. By the way, I hope you're not attached to the floor in that space, because I was looking at it again this morning when I went over to fix the front window and it's got to come out too, no doubt about it."

"Take it all," I said with a laugh. "I just want it to look and feel like a real bakery."

"You got it," Lois said, tucking her notebook away. "Tomorrow morning I want to get over there and do final measurements, then the next day we should be good to go. We can order equipment tomorrow after I get the measurements too, if you want help with that."

I nodded gratefully. "I'm totally in over my head here, so any help would be great."

As Lois rolled up her sketches and set them aside, I leaned back in my chair, the warmth of the bread lingering in the air. Something about the all the things that had happened gnawed at me, and I decided to ask.

"Do you know much about Wyatt Parker?" I said casually, though my curiosity was anything but.

Lois looked up, her eyebrows raised. "Wyatt? What about him?"

"He showed up at the shop after I bailed Vince out the night after we found Marcus," I said, recalling the confrontation. "He seemed... angry. Something about Vince not selling the space to him after all."

Lois snorted, crossing her arms. "Sounds like Wyatt. He's been circling that property for years, trying to get Vince to sell. Probably thinks he can flip it or turn it into another one of his cash cows. Wyatt's got his hands in a lot of things around here—real estate, construction, even a bar on the boardwalk."

"So who is he?" I asked. "Besides a real estate mogul with an attitude."

"Wyatt went to high school with us all," Lois said, her voice taking on a contemplative tone. "He and Marcus were friends back then, actually—or as close to friends as two jerks can be. Thick as thieves, always getting into trouble." She frowned, drumming her fingers on the table. "It's funny, though. I can't picture them reconnecting now. Not after all these years."

"Why not?"

"Because they went their separate ways fast after high school. Marcus left town, and Wyatt stuck around, building his little empire here. I doubt they've spoken since. But..." She hesitated, glancing at me. "It does make you wonder. If Marcus came back, did he and Wyatt cross paths? It's kinda weird that Marcus was killed in Vince's shop that he's been after for so long."

The comment sent a ripple of unease through me, but I pushed it aside, focusing on another thread that had been tugging at me since Fran's comment in the diner. "You mentioned Alma the other day," I said carefully. "What's the story there? Is there any connection between Marcus or Wyatt?"

Lois's face darkened, her usual lighthearted demeanor

fading. She nodded slowly. "Alma Ramirez. Sweetest girl in the world. Everyone loved her." She sighed, shaking her head. "She disappeared right before graduation. Just vanished one night. They never found her."

"Do people think Marcus had anything to do with it?" I asked, leaning forward.

Lois hesitated, her gaze dropping to the table. "Some people did. He skipped town not long after, which looked bad, I guess. But there was never any proof. The cops poked around, asked questions, but nothing stuck. It's been fifteen years, and no one really talks about it anymore. Too painful for the folks who were close to her."

Her words hung in the air and I thought about all the possibilities.

Lois shook her head, her expression unreadable. "I don't know why Marcus came back after all this time. But he must've had a reason. And now he's dead." She met my gaze, her eyes serious. "Whatever that reason was, it's not just a coincidence. It can't be."

I nodded, her words sinking in as my mind spun with questions. Had Marcus and Wyatt seen each other? Could they have been hiding something about Alma all these years? And if so, had it finally caught up with them?

Lois glanced around the room, her sharp eyes zeroing in on the chipped paint on the windowsill and the uneven floorboards. "This place has potential," she said with a grin, "but man, it's seen better days."

I laughed, following her gaze. "You don't have to tell me. Half the time I feel like I'm living inside a dust bunny."

"You know," Lois said, tapping her chin, "a little elbow grease and some new fixtures could make this place really nice. Paint those cabinets, refinish the floors, maybe swap out that leaky faucet. I bet you'd fall in love with it."

"I know, right? That was the idea when I moved here, to be honest. I planned to fix this place up and sell it. But somehow I convinced myself to start a bakery, instead," I said with a laugh and then shook my head. "But one project at a time, I guess. I've got all my energy focused on the bakery now that I decided to do it, so the bungalow will have to wait." I wondered, too, if I wasn't putting the bungalow work off because in my heart I knew I really wanted to stay in Moonstone Bay, not flip this little place.

"Fair enough," Lois said with a grin. "But if you need a hand when you get to it, let me know. I'm great at demo work."

I smiled, appreciating her easygoing offer. "I'll keep that in mind."

Lois stood and stretched, Princess watching her from the couch with a look that could only be described as pure laziness. "Thanks for the bread. I needed that," she said, patting her stomach. "I'll swing by the shop first thing in the morning to get started. Let Vince know we're coming."

I nodded, then hesitated. "I'll text him."

Lois raised an eyebrow, her grin turning sly. "Text him, huh? Not call?"

Heat crept up my neck, and I tried to play it cool. "It's just easier."

"Sure it is," Lois said, her tone teasing but not unkind.

Before I could respond, she clapped her hands and called, "Princess! Time to go!"

Princess didn't move. She let out a deep, dramatic sigh, her head flopping onto her paws as if the very thought of leaving was too much effort.

"Princess," Lois said again, more sternly this time.

The dog didn't budge.

I bit back a laugh as Lois groaned. "She's the boss of me, you know that? Come on, girl, don't make me look bad."

At last, Princess heaved herself off the couch and padded toward the door, her tail wagging lazily. Shorty watched her go, flicking his own tail.

Lois rolled her eyes, but couldn't hide her affection. "See you tomorrow, Ginny. And hey—try not to let this bakery project drive you nuts, alright?"

"I'll try," I said with a laugh. "Thanks, Lois. For everything."

Lois waved as she and Princess disappeared down the path, leaving me alone in the quiet bungalow.

13

The next day, I met Lois bright and early down on the boardwalk. Shortcake strutted along beside me, his tail held high like a flag. His determined pace made it clear he was not about to be left behind again and that he knew exactly where we were going. I sighed, thinking about the yowling fit he'd thrown when I tried to leave him at the bungalow earlier.

Lois leaned casually against a lamppost as I got close to the shop, two cups of coffee in her hands. She grinned and held them up as she caught sight of me. "Thought we could use a little liquid fuel for this thing," she called, lifting one of the cups in a salute.

"You're a lifesaver," I said, taking the offered cup. The warmth seeped into my hands as I took a grateful sip.

She stooped to give Shorty a long pet, which he accepted with grace, winding through her legs to show how happy he was with the attention. She grinned, scratching behind his ears. "This guy's got more swagger than most people I know. You should let him handle the negotiations with the suppliers."

"I think he's already handling my schedule," I muttered, watching Shortcake preen under her attention.

We walked to the shop together, and I pushed open the unlocked door. "Vince said he'd be here this morning," I said as we stepped inside and tried to ignore the thudding in my chest as I thought about my scruffy but lovable landlord.

Sure enough, Vince was behind his desk, tapping at his laptop with the expression of someone losing an argument with technology. His desk was a clutter of papers, a coffee cup, and what looked like a half-empty box of old Chinese food.

"Hey, Ginny, Lois," he said, glancing up with a tired smile. But his face lit up when he spotted Shortcake trotting in behind us. "There's my guy!"

Shortcake leapt onto Vince's desk with the grace of a cat who knew he was welcome. He circled once, then settled himself directly on top of a stack of papers, purring loudly.

"You really have a way with cats," I said, crossing my arms. "Shorty barely tolerated my ex, but he's already got you wrapped around his paw."

"Can you blame him?" Vince said, scratching Shortcake's chin. The cat stretched luxuriously, clearly in heaven.

Lois chuckled, shaking her head. "Well, it's nice to see you haven't changed much, Vince. Still charming the city folk, I see."

He laughed as he stroked the cat's back, and I couldn't help but love how easily the two of them were bonding. His blue eyes sparkled, and a dimpled, boyish grin appeared. "You'll always be Chicken Wing to me," he whispered to the cat, who purred even louder.

I turned to Lois, taking a sip of my coffee. "Alright, where do we start?"

Lois pulled a rolled-up sketch from under her arm and looked around the room for a place to put it. "Hey, Vince, you mind?" she asked him as she held up the plans and glanced toward his messy desk. "I wouldn't ask, but..."

His sigh was overly loud, but he grabbed the takeout and a handful of folders and threw them on the ground next to him. Shortcake eyed it all, but didn't move from his perch. The cat wasn't going to give us an inch.

Lois grinned. "Thanks," she said as she spread the plans across Vince's cluttered desk on the other side of the cat. "First things first—exact measurements. We'll figure out exactly how much space you've got to work with for the ovens, counters, and sinks."

"Hold up," Vince said, raising an eyebrow as he peered over at the plans. "Ovens, counters, sinks? You're talking about tearing this place apart."

"Uh, yeah. That's kind of the point," I said, leaning over to look more closely at the sketch, trying to ignore the mesmerizing sandalwood scent that drifted from Vince. "Hard to have a bakery without making some changes in here."

He frowned but didn't say anything else, and I turned my attention back to Lois, pointing to a spot on the plan. "This corner would be perfect for a display case. And over here," I gestured to another area, "a cozy spot for a couple of tables. People could grab coffee and linger."

Vince snorted, his chair creaking as he leaned back. "Yeah, because nothing screams 'cozy' like eating muffins next to a P.I. interrogating someone about a cheating spouse."

Lois grinned, clearly enjoying the dynamic. "Hey, you could offer a combo deal. Coffee, a scone, and relationship advice."

"Very funny," Vince said, but his lips twitched with amusement. "But seriously, guys. How are we going to make this work?"

I crossed my arms, raising an eyebrow. It was a little late to be having this conversation. I decided to take a different tack.

"Do you actually *have* clients? From what *I've* seen, your main clients are stray cats and old Chinese takeout."

Lois let out a loud laugh, while Vince just gave me a flat look.

"Seriously, Vince. Do you have regular clients or something? How do you get work?"

Vince turned his gaze back to the computer, suddenly squinting at something and not meeting my eye. "Uh. I guess everybody kind of knows me around here. So when they need a P.I. they come to me."

"Do you get a lot of business?"

He crossed his arms and leaned back in his rickety chair with a frown. "What is this? What's with the questions?"

"Jeez, I'm just curious! And maybe wondering how we're going to make the whole P.I. slash bakery thing work." I was angry at myself as much as him that I didn't think to work these details out before I'd gotten into the renovations and dreaming phase of this project. Now that we were having the conversation, I had a whole lot of doubts about whether this would even work.

He leaned back in his chair, and it squeaked loudly. I worried it might fall apart as he sat there, but it held out as he began to squeakily rock back and forth.

"I'm not saying it's a bad idea," Vince said slowly, his chair creaking with each exaggerated rock, "but I'm not exactly running a bakery-friendly operation here. You really think my clients are gonna feel comfortable walking into a shop that smells like cinnamon buns and has people sitting around sipping lattes?"

"Okay, first of all," I said, trying not to let my frustration show, "how dare you insult cinnamon buns? And second, I'm open to ideas. But we have to figure out a way to make this work, because I'm not backing out of this bakery. I've already invested too much…" Not money so much, I realized. But I'd invested a whole heap of dreams and future plans into this thing and I was already very attached.

Lois held up her hands, a grin spreading across her face. "Alright, kids, simmer down. Let's not forget we've got the perfect solution right here: me and my hammer," she said.

Vince gave her a skeptical look. "And what's the brilliant plan, Wheeler?"

"Partitioned office," Lois said without missing a beat. "We build you a little space back here in the corner. Put up nice soundproof walls, maybe even add a back door for your clients so they don't have to come through the main bakery." She pointed to the back of the blueprint where she sketched in her ideas. "That way, you keep your business separate, Ginny gets her bakery, and everyone's happy."

I tilted my head, looking at the sketch. "That… could actually work."

Vince rubbed his chin, clearly not convinced. "What about cost? Soundproofing's not cheap. And where are my clients supposed to park?"

Lois rolled her eyes. "It's Moonstone Bay, Vince, not L.A. They can park wherever they want. As for the cost, Ginny here has already agreed to pay for renovations, right?"

I hesitated, feeling Vince's gaze shift to me. "I mean, yeah. I'm covering the *bakery* renovations. I guess adding an office wouldn't be a huge stretch… as long as I can use it as an office sometimes, too."

"Fair enough," he said after a minute of staring us both down, leaning forward to glance at the blueprint. "But if we're doing this, I get to pick the color of the walls. None of that pastel cupcake crap."

"Deal," I said, biting back a smile.

Lois clapped her hands, beaming. "See? That wasn't so hard.

Now, let's get to work before you two find something else to bicker about." She pulled out her measuring tape, giving the shop a critical once-over. "Alright, Ginny, let's talk colors and flooring while I take these measurements. You have anything in mind?"

"I was thinking light, airy—maybe some soft blues or greens. Something to play off the coastal vibe." I glanced at the worn decades old flooring. "And definitely something durable for the floors. This place is going to see a lot of foot traffic."

"Good call," Lois said, jotting down notes on her clipboard.

Vince cleared his throat loudly from his desk, where he'd opened his laptop again. "Remember, I've got a say in the color!"

"You've got a say in the color of the office space, not the bakery," I shot back.

"Fine, but I'm begging, please, no seashell patterns," he replied. "I can't take it. I'll go crazy."

"I'm in full agreement there. No seashells."

Shortcake stretched on Vince's desk, his tail flicking lazily before he settled down again. Vince gave him an absent scratch behind the ears as he turned back to his computer, and I shook my head with a small smile.

As Lois and I hashed out ideas for counters and paint, I felt a flicker of excitement bubble up in me. It wasn't just the bakery or the progress we were making—it was the way this strange little team was starting to come together.

Even if Vince didn't realize it yet, we were all in this thing together now.

14

A little while later, as Lois and I finished sketching ideas for the bakery layout, Vince's growl of frustration broke the quiet hum of activity.

"Are you kidding me?" he snapped, smacking the desk with his palm hard enough to make Shortcake leap up, fur puffed in indignation.

Lois and I both turned toward him, startled. Vince let out a heavy sigh, dragging a hand through his already-messy hair.

"If I can't figure out why Marcus was in this shop, I'm toast," he muttered, slumping back in his chair.

The tension in his voice pulled at me. I could tell he was starting to lose faith, which wasn't good.

"What are your theories?" I asked him as I moved closer, ready to help.

He let out a grunt and folded his arms over his chest. I tried not to notice the way his biceps bulged. "Oh, no. I don't need any input from the bakery department."

Before I could respond, Lois beat me to it, snapping her measuring tape back with a sharp clack. "Alright, Rinaldi, enough with the martyr act. Let us help you."

Vince gave her a sidelong look. "Help me? You're a contractor, Lois. Unless you're planning to build me a clue, I don't see how you're gonna fix this."

She rolled her eyes, crossing her arms. "I know this town better than you do, Mr. Hotshot P.I. And in case that isn't enough, you've got Ginny here. Did you know she's a criminal defense attorney?"

His head snapped up, his blue eyes narrowing as they shifted to me. "You're a lawyer?"

I felt myself flush under the weight of his scrutiny. "I'm not practicing right now..." Obviously.

Vince raised an eyebrow. "And now you're opening a bakery?"

I bristled at his tone, but kept my voice even. "People can do more than one thing, you know. Anyway, the point is, I've handled plenty of cases like this before. I know how to think through evidence. You want to figure out why Marcus was here? Let me help."

His lips pressed into a thin line as he seemed to weigh my words. The silence stretched, the only sound the distant tapping of Shortcake's claws as he hopped back onto Vince's desk, apparently forgiving him for the earlier scare.

"Don't be an idiot, Vince," Lois said bluntly. "You've been banging your head against this thing all day, and it's getting you nowhere. Let us help you out."

Vince exhaled, the tension in his shoulders softening ever so slightly. "Fine," he said finally, though his tone was reluctant. "But don't say I didn't warn you. This whole thing's a mess."

He stood and moved to the back corner of the room, dragging out two folding chairs that looked like they'd seen better days. "Might as well get comfortable," he said, plopping one down in front of his desk and motioning for me to take the other.

I tested the chair cautiously, half expecting it to collapse under me. "Wow," I said, arching an eyebrow. "Maybe we should set aside a little money for proper furniture. I can't believe you let your clients sit on these."

"Might be why he doesn't have many clients," Lois added as she sat on the edge of one of the rusty metal chairs next to me.

"Alright, are you two gonna help or criticize me all day long? Because I can't take it. I just can't."

I softened, hearing the frustration, the pain, and the fear in his tone. "Sorry. We're going to help."

Vince leaned back in his creaky desk chair, scrubbing a hand over his face. "Alright, where do we even start? The guy shows up out of nowhere, ends up dead in my office, and now I'm the one getting grilled by the cops. None of it makes sense."

"Let's go back to the beginning," I said, settling into the wobbly chair. "Lois and I had a talk about Wyatt Parker yesterday. She said he and Marcus were friends in high school."

Vince's mouth twisted, his eyes narrowing. "Yeah, that's true. Wyatt was always dragging Marcus into trouble. They were constantly together until Marcus skipped town after graduation."

"You think he could have killed Marcus?"

He crossed his arms and gazed out toward the front of the shop. "I doubt it. Why would he do that?"

"He wanted to buy this place badly enough to bail you out, right?" I replied. "Maybe there's something in this shop that Marcus knew about—something Wyatt wants."

Vince's gaze flicked to the walls of the room, his expression skeptical. "What could possibly be here? This place is a dump and totally empty. It's been in my family forever, but there's nothing special about it."

"Doesn't mean there wasn't at some point," Lois pointed

out. "People hide stuff all the time. Money, documents... secrets. Who knows?"

The three of us scanned the space with new interest, but there was absolutely nothing to see other than old floors and water-stained ceiling tiles. I had no idea how anything could be hidden here unless it was in the walls or the ceiling.

I turned to Vince. "You had no idea that Marcus was here the night he died?"

His face blushed bright crimson, and he turned back to his computer. "Nah. Like I told Donovan, I was drunk." He turned back and met my gaze. "As much as I hate to admit it, I was dead to the world from about eight that night until I woke up to everyone in my shop the next day."

I nodded slowly. "It's just so strange, you know? That he would show up out of the blue, talk to Beth, and then come over here with a hammer and get shot."

"Wait, he talked to Beth?" Vince asked, sitting up straighter.

"Yeah, she was outside the day it happened. Told us Marcus came to see her that night, that she told him about their son and that he left in a huff and she never saw him again," Lois replied.

Vince frowned. "I bet that was a shock for him. To find out about the kid."

"I'm wondering more about Wyatt," I said. "Why is he so desperate to buy this shop? And why does Marcus end up dead here, of all places?"

Vince frowned and shot a glance at Lois. "You think this has to do with Alma?"

The name sent a shiver down my spine, and Lois nodded grimly.

"It's a possibility," she said. "Alma disappeared right before graduation, and people always suspected Marcus knew more than he let on. Maybe Wyatt knew something about Marcus. Or Marcus knew something about Wyatt..."

"Do *you* think Wyatt could've killed Marcus?" I asked her.

Lois raised an eyebrow. "I'm not saying for sure he did, but he's definitely got a temper. And if Marcus was back here stirring up the past—especially anything to do with Alma—Wyatt wouldn't be thrilled about it."

"Why's that?" I asked, feeling like I was missing something.

Lois and Vince glanced at one another. "Wyatt had a thing for Alma back in the day. She never wanted him though, and I think it really made Wyatt crazy that he couldn't have her."

I sat back and processed this. "Did the police look into Wyatt for Alma's disappearance?"

Vince nodded. "Some, but they focused more on Marcus because he left town. Nothing came of it, though." Vince leaned forward, resting his arms on the desk. "The thing I'm trying to figure out is, why here? If Marcus wanted to pick a fight with Wyatt, why not go to him directly? Why show up at my shop with a hammer?"

"I keep coming back to that," I said. "Why this place? Why the hammer? It doesn't make sense."

Lois tapped her fingers on the table, her expression thoughtful. "Maybe he wasn't looking for a fight. Maybe he was looking for answers. But what kind of answers, and why now?"

The room fell silent as we all mulled it over. Shortcake, still perched on Vince's desk, stretched lazily before settling back down, his tail flicking against a pile of papers.

"Marcus talked to Beth before he died," I said finally. "And we know he went to her house before coming here. That has to mean something. Maybe something he found out from Beth made him come here."

"Or maybe Beth told him something about Wyatt," Lois

suggested. "If Wyatt was tied to Alma's disappearance, Marcus might've been trying to figure out how it all fit together."

"Beth said he left her house angry," I pointed out. "Maybe he found out something he didn't like—or maybe he thought coming here would somehow fix things."

Vince sighed, leaning back in his chair. "So, what? We're saying Marcus had some big revelation, came here to... what? Hide? Dig something up from the past? Make some grand gesture? And then Wyatt followed him and shot him?"

"It's possible," I said slowly. "But it's also possible we're missing something. Maybe Marcus wasn't trying to fix anything at all. Maybe he was just running from something—or someone."

The tension in the room hung heavy as we all considered the possibilities. Whatever had driven Marcus back to Moonstone Bay, it was clear he hadn't shared his plans with anyone —or, if he had, they weren't talking.

The weight of the conversation settled over us all as we grew quiet. Even Shortcake seemed unusually still, his green eyes flicking between us like he was following every word.

Vince broke the silence with a long sigh, leaning forward and resting his elbows on the desk. I recognized fatigue and knew it was a good time for us all to take a break. Glancing at Vince's gaunt face, I wondered when the man had eaten last.

"These are all interesting lines of thought, but I think we all need to take a break, get some rest, get some food. And then maybe regroup on it all in the morning?"

Lois nodded and stood from the rickety chair. "That sounds good to me," she said as she grabbed the plans and tools she had scattered about. "I'll think on this, maybe ask some questions around, see if anything knows any more than they're letting on."

"Same here," Vince said as he stood and stretched. He

caught me staring at him and gave me an adorable, lopsided grin.

I blushed and cleared my throat. "Do you need anything? Food? Money?" I asked him as Lois waved us goodbye.

His smile disappeared. "Nah, I'm fine. You've already done a lot for me and I appreciate it."

"Alright," I said, feeling the blush creep up my neck again. "But if you do need something, just... don't be too proud to ask, okay?"

Vince's lips quirked into that lopsided grin again, softer this time. "I'll keep that in mind."

I lingered for a moment, watching him as he scratched behind Shortcake's ears. The sight made my chest ache, though I wasn't sure why. Maybe it was the exhaustion etched into his features, or the way he kept trying to shoulder everything alone. Or maybe it was the nagging thought in the back of my mind that Vince wasn't just a puzzle I wanted to solve—he was someone I wanted to believe in.

"See you later, Vince," I said finally, my voice quieter than I intended, as I motioned for Shorty to follow me.

"See you later, Ginny," he replied, his tone equally subdued.

As I stepped out onto the boardwalk, Shortcake trotted along at my heels, his tail flicking with contentment. There were very few people around at this time of day, and I clearly heard the distant sound of waves breaking against the shore. I glanced back at the shop, its dim light spilling onto the weathered planks outside, and couldn't shake the feeling that whatever Marcus had been running from, it wasn't finished.

With a deep breath, I turned toward home, my mind already spinning with questions I couldn't yet answer. But one thing was certain: I wasn't walking away from this—not from the bakery, not from Vince, and not from the truth.

15

The next morning I woke up stiff and cramped, my eyes puffier than I would have liked. Morning sunlight filtered through my kitchen window as I stumbled into the small space. I winced as I took in the absolute chaos I'd left behind the night before. Mixing bowls, measuring spoons, and flour-covered countertops made it look like a baking bomb had gone off.

Shortcake sat on the edge of the counter, flicking his tail disapprovingly as if he were the kitchen supervisor and I'd failed an inspection. "Yeah, yeah, I'll clean it up later," I muttered, stifling a yawn.

I glanced at the clock and winced. I'd stayed up far too late testing cookie recipes—chocolate chip, oatmeal raisin, a questionable attempt at white chocolate macadamia. The results were all edible, but none of them screamed "signature item" to me.

Pouring myself a glass of orange juice, I leaned against the counter and considered what opening day at the bakery might look like. How many items would I need to start with? Should I focus on pastries or throw in some savory options too? And what about coffee? The idea of ordering an espresso machine had crossed my mind—not just for the shop but for myself. There wasn't exactly a Starbucks around the corner, and Fran's coffee was fine here and there. But having spent most of my life in San Francisco with plenty of money, I'd grown accustomed to a certain type of coffee and I knew I'd start going through withdrawals if I waited much longer.

With a sigh, I decided to push the coffee dilemma to the back burner. I had bigger things to focus on today, like meeting Lois at the shop to finalize equipment plans.

I got dressed quickly and threw on some makeup, then debated whether or not to bring Shorty with me to the shop. I knew I would probably have to leave him at home once the place opened. I doubted the health inspector would take kindly to a cat mascot. So I decided to bring him along for as long as he was able to come without causing trouble.

The walk to the shop was brisk, the salty sea air waking me up better than any caffeine could. Shortcake trotted along beside me with purpose. I waved to a couple of people I recognized, almost feeling like I was becoming a local.

The boardwalk was still waking up, shop owners flipping signs to "Open" and sweeping their stoops. I gave a polite wave to Fran through the window of the diner as I passed. She gave me a curt nod and then turned back to a customer. I wondered if the woman would ever see me as part of the town, or forever think of me as the city girl. Only time would tell.

When I reached the shop, I fumbled with the keys Vince had given me the day before. It felt strangely significant, unlocking the door and stepping into what I was beginning to think of as *my* space.

Inside, the air was cool and faintly dusty, the smell of old wood mingling with the salty tang that seemed to cling to everything in Moonstone Bay. I paused, taking a moment to daydream about what the space would look like when it was finished: glass display cases filled with pastries, cheerful customers seated at tables, and the warm, comforting aroma of fresh-baked bread filling the air.

Shortcake meowed impatiently, pulling me out of my reverie. "Alright, boss," I said with a chuckle. "Let's get to work."

I'd brought my laptop with me so I could do a little bit of research and order some things while Lois worked and I moved over to Vince's desk, eyeing the mess skeptically, before putting my laptop on top of a pile of bills.

Shortly after I'd settled in and gotten lost in my ever-widening hunt of bakery equipment, the front door creaked open. Lois walked in, holding a clipboard in one hand and gesturing over her shoulder with the other.

"C'mon, Jackson, hustle up!" she called.

A lanky college-aged guy followed her in, balancing a large toolbox and a sledgehammer with an ease that made me feel weak and incompetent.

"Morning," Lois said cheerfully, giving Shortcake a quick pet as he sauntered over to investigate. "Ready for us to do some damage?"

"Absolutely," I said, laughing as I gestured toward the wall they'd be working on.

Lois glanced at my laptop, raising an eyebrow. "I would love to say we won't make much noise, but that would be a big fat lie. Hope we don't break your concentration too bad."

I laughed and waved her away. "Law school taught me to tone everything out. Don't worry about it. But let me know if you need any help!"

She nodded and then turned to her companion. "Jackson, buddy. Let's get to it, yeah? Why don't we start on that back wall and see what we're working with."

The sharp clink of tools hitting the floor made Shortcake's ears flick back, and he darted back to my side, curling up on Vince's desk as if he'd claimed it.

The front door opened a little while later and I glanced up from my laptop as Vince stepped in, looking marginally more put together than he had the day before, though the circles under his eyes betrayed how little rest he'd gotten.

"Morning," he muttered as he walked into the space. His eyes landed on me, sitting at his desk, and his brows furrowed.

"Comfortable?" he asked, a wry smile tugging at the corners of his mouth.

"Very," I replied, not bothering to hide my grin. "You should try it sometime. You look like you could use some sleep."

"Funny," he shot back, though the slight twitch of his lips made me think he wasn't as annoyed as he pretended to be.

Shortcake perked up at the sound of Vince's voice and stretched lazily before hopping down from the desk to wind around Vince's legs. Vince crouched to scratch the cat behind the ears, his expression softening.

"Hey there, friend," he said to Shortcake.

Lois, standing near the back wall with her clipboard, waved at Vince. "Well, now the gang's all here. How cozy."

Vince straightened, rubbing the back of his neck. "What are you guys even doing back there?"

"Demo," Lois said simply, twirling her pencil between her fingers.

"Demo?" Vince repeated. "You aren't going to ruin my office space, are you? This space is all I've got, ladies."

"She's starting on the renovations," I said, gesturing to the plans on the desk. "You know, so I can actually have a functioning bakery in here someday. Don't worry, Vince, Lois knows what she's doing."

"Right," Vince muttered, his gaze flicking between Lois and Jackson as they set to work.

I rolled my eyes. "Look, I promise to pay to put it all back to its glorious, dilapidated state if things don't work out."

He grinned at that and then his eyes shifted to the desk—specifically, to my laptop perched amidst his chaotic pile of papers. He gave me a look that was part amused, part exasperated. "You know, this is my desk, right?"

I glanced at the clutter around my laptop and smirked. "Oh, is that what this is? I thought it was some kind of archaeological dig site."

He chuckled a moment, then grew straight faced as he ran a hand through his hair. "Seriously, lady. I need to get to work."

I doubted he had much work to do, but it *was* his desk. "Five more minutes?" I begged.

He grinned, pulling up the rickety chair with a theatrical creak. "Alright, pastry queen, you keep on shopping or whatever you're doing over there. I'll just take up this little corner and wait to figure out who killed Marcus."

I hesitated, then sighed dramatically and started gathering my things. "Fine, you win. But we're definitely getting another desk in here. Or maybe two, because this thing feels like it's held together with duct tape and a prayer."

Vince leaned back with an exaggerated sigh. "You won't get any argument here."

I raised an eyebrow, shooting him a playful glare. "I better not."

Lois, watching the whole exchange, rolled her eyes. "You two are ridiculous. Let me know when you're done playing house so we can actually get some work done."

The sharp thud of a hammer against drywall jolted us all out of our conversation as Jackson swung and connected with a big piece of the back wall. Bits of plaster and old paint chips scattered onto the floor, and I cringed at the mess.

"Here we go," Lois said, stepping back to let Jackson do his thing. "Nice swing, man."

Jackson raised the sledgehammer to swing again, but then paused, frowning at something in the wall. "Uh... Lois? You might want to take a look at this."

"What is it?" Lois asked, moving closer.

"I'm not sure," Jackson replied, pointing to a small hollowed-out section within the wall. "But it doesn't look like part of the building."

Vince and I perked up and watched as Lois went over and leaned in, her eyes narrowing as she inspected the space. Then she froze, her face shifting from curiosity to something much more serious. "Oh, you've got to be kidding me," she muttered.

"What?" I asked, my pulse quickening as I stood up and moved closer. Vince came up behind me and we all peered into the gaping hole in the wall.

At first, what I saw didn't make sense—just a dull metallic shape against the wooden frame. Then the pieces clicked together in my mind and I froze.

It was a gun.

The thing was mostly wrapped in cloth, but the end was sticking out and between that and the outline of a gun, it was clear what it was.

Vince's expression darkened as he took in the sight. "Fantastic," he muttered, running a hand through his hair. "Just what I need."

"Is that... real?" I asked, my voice quieter than I'd intended.

"Looks like it," Lois said grimly. "Old, though. Rusted, from the looks of it."

I leaned in closer and saw the signs of rust on the edge of

the metal that was visible. A million possibilities suddenly ran through my mind.

"Remember how Marcus had a hammer in his hand when we found him dead?" I said, excitement lacing my words. I started to pace. "I thought that was so strange. But you know what? I bet he was here to knock out this wall and take this gun! Maybe that was even why he was killed!"

Vince's jaw tightened, his gaze fixed on the gun. He nodded slowly and then turned to me, his eyes bright with excitement. "Which means whoever killed him probably knew about this, too."

"If that was why he was here. And if that was why he was killed. Then yeah, that makes a lot of sense. But that's also a lot of ifs."

Lois nodded, her expression serious. "It is, but they are ifs that make an awful lot of sense. Here's one more if for you—if this thing's connected to Marcus's death, the cops are going to want to see it."

I pulled out my phone, already dialing.

"They'll want to arrest me again, is what they'll want to do," Vince muttered bitterly as I connected to the dispatcher.

I glanced at him, my chest tightening at the defeated tone in his voice. "Sorry," I mouthed before turning to the phone and telling the dispatcher what we'd found.

16

After I called the police, we waited in a strained silence that made the small space feel even smaller. Vince leaned against his desk, arms crossed tightly over his chest, his gaze fixed on the hole in the wall like he might jump up any minute and try to fill it back in. Lois perched on the edge of one of the folding chairs, spinning her hammer idly, her face calm but her movements tense. Even Jackson, seemingly unbothered by much, quietly stood by the wall with the sledgehammer at his feet, watching for the first crack of drama.

I sat on the edge of Vince's desk, processing what I knew—or thought I knew—about the gun. How long had it been in the wall? And who had put it there? If it was connected to Marcus, did that mean this gun had some part to play in his murder, or was it just a coincidence? The possibilities ran through my brain faster than I could make sense of them. I was used to piecing things together after the fact, not in the middle of the chaos. The discovery of the gun challenged everything I knew as a lawyer.

Shortcake broke the silence with a loud yawn and stretched

across Vince's papers like he had no clue the world was imploding around us. I scratched his ears absently, finding some comfort in his soft fur, but the quiet dragged on, pressing down on me. Vince fiddled with his key ring and didn't make eye contact. This had to be hard for him, having already been fingered in Marcus' murder. Now the shop he owned had a gun buried in the wall. Who knew what Sheriff Donovan would make of it all or what kind of trouble Vince might be in this time around?

The faint sound of boots on the boardwalk outside broke the quiet. I straightened, my heart giving a nervous thud as the noise grew louder. The door creaked open as Sheriff Donovan stepped in, his khaki uniform as crisp as his demeanor. A younger deputy followed, carrying a camera and notebook, his wide-eyed expression suggesting this might be his first real call of significance.

Donovan's sharp gaze swept the room, taking in each of us before settling on the hole in the wall. "The dispatcher said you all found a gun?" His voice was level, but there was an edge to it that made me nervous.

"We sure did," Lois said, still gripping the hammer. She gestured toward the gap in the wall. "Jackson and I were doing some demo work, opening up space for new piping when— bam—there it was." We all jumped as she said the bam part and I gave a little nervous laugh and then reached out to pet Shortcake as I eyed the rest of the room.

The sheriff's eyes narrowed slightly as he stepped further into the room, his boots heavy on the worn floorboards. "Demo work, huh? For the bakery, I take it?"

I nodded, feeling a pang of unease, and glanced toward Vince, who looked like he'd rather be anywhere else. His jaw was tight, his blue eyes fixed on the wall and avoiding Donovan's gaze.

"Let's see what we've got," he said lightly.

"Just so you know," Vince muttered, finally ready to say something, "I didn't put it there. If that's what you're thinking."

Donovan's gaze flicked to him for a moment before turning back to the wall. "Not thinking anything yet, Rinaldi. Just gathering facts."

The tension was thick, and I cleared my throat as I stepped forward. "None of us touched the gun—it's still exactly how it was when we found it."

Donovan nodded curtly, his attention turning to the younger deputy. "Go ahead and get pictures before we do anything else."

"Yes, sir," the deputy said, stepping forward and snapping photos with a shaky hand.

I shifted my weight, feeling the strain of the charged atmosphere. My gaze darted to Lois, who stood with her hands on her hips, clearly unbothered by the sheriff's presence. Vince, on the other hand, looked like he was waiting for the other shoe to drop, his discomfort radiating off him in waves.

Donovan's lips tightened as he stepped closer to inspect the hole and the space around it once the officer was done with the pictures, hands on his hips. "Any other work been done on this place recently?" His question was sharp, and his gaze landed squarely on Vince.

"Not since my parents owned it," Vince replied, straightening defensively. "They renovated the office back when I was in high school. This wall's been here ever since, as far as I know."

Donovan grunted, nodding as if filing the information away. "Alright." He pulled a pair of gloves from his pocket and tugged them on with practiced efficiency. "Let's see what we're dealing with."

We all leaned forward as the sheriff reached into the hole,

careful and deliberate. When he withdrew his hand, he held the gun wrapped partially in an old rag. The bit of the gun that stuck out glinted dully in the dim shop light as he placed it in an evidence bag.

"Looks like a standard revolver," Donovan said, weighing it in his gloved hand before passing it to the deputy. "But we'll have to take it back to the lab before we know more."

The deputy continued snapping pictures of the wall and space around as Donovan turned back to us. "You all have any idea how long it's been in there?"

"Like I said," Vince replied, his voice tense, "this wall's been standing since my parents redid the place. That was... I dunno, fifteen years ago? Maybe longer."

"So no recent work? No one else has been poking around here before now?"

"Not a soul," Vince said firmly, but his jaw tightened again, and I wondered if he was thinking about Marcus.

Donovan exhaled sharply, his gaze drifting back to the wall. "I hate to be the bearer of bad news, but we're gonna have to shut this place down a while longer, have another look around."

I groaned, and Jackson shrugged and picked up the sledge-hammer, already heading to the door.

"Any idea how long it might take?" I asked.

Sheriff Donovan frowned. "Hard to say, but the afternoon, at least." His face softened. "We'll try to get through it quickly... and make as little mess as possible. I'll give you a call when we're finished."

I hesitated, exchanging a glance with Lois before mentioning the next bit. "I heard about the girl Alma, who disappeared a while back. Do you think that gun has anything to do with her?"

Donovan's gaze snapped to me, his expression sharpening. "The Ramirez case?" He was silent for a beat, then said carefully, "It's a possibility, but I doubt it. Her disappearance's still classified as a missing person's case, but there's been no movement on it in years. Most folks assumed she left town."

Vince frowned, his brow furrowing as he crossed his arms. "She *did* disappear around the time my parents were renovating this place," he said, his tone thoughtful. "I can't remember exactly when, but I could probably dig up some records or bills to get the dates, see for sure if it was around the same time. My bigger question is, does it have to do with Marcus?"

Sheriff Donovan eyed him cooly. "I'm not sure, son. Do you have a reason to think it does?"

Vince held up his hands and blew out a breath. "Nope! Just speculating!"

I frowned and tried to put pieces together. If Alma's disappearance and this gun were connected, it meant this quiet little office-bakery space might be at the center of something far darker than any of us had imagined.

Donovan's gaze lingered on Vince a beat longer than felt necessary before he nodded. "Alright. Whatever the reason the gun was here, and whether it's connected to Marcus or Alma or not, I still need to process this space one more time. So if y'all don't mind..."

Vince pushed off the desk with a shrug, and Lois and I started to follow him to the door.

The sheriff called after us just before we left. "You got nothing to hide, right Rinaldi?"

Vince turned back to look at the sheriff, fire in his gaze. "Of course I've got nothing to hide. Never did, Donovan."

"Okay. And I'm sure I don't need to remind you that leaving town is a hard no."

Vince frowned and crossed his arms like he wanted to backtalk, but the sheriff's gaze shifted to me. "You've got a knack for asking the right questions, Ms. Malone. Let's hope your curiosity doesn't land *you* in trouble."

I swallowed hard, offering a tight smile. "I'll keep that in mind."

We gathered our things quickly and headed out, letting the police once again take over my bakery.

17

Lois let out a low whistle as we all stepped out into the late afternoon sunshine. "Well," she said, adjusting her tool belt, "looks like we've got ourselves a full-blown mess."

"No kidding," Vince muttered, his voice rough. He crossed his arms over his chest, his gaze flicking toward the choppy ocean, then back to me. "That guy's got it out for me. You know that, right?"

I raised an eyebrow, crossing my arms. "He's just doing his job, Vince."

"He's doing his job all right," he grunted, his tone dripping with sarcasm. "Feels more like he's waiting for me to slip up so he can slap those cuffs on me again."

"You don't have anything to hide," I pointed out, sharper than I intended. "So stop acting like you do."

Lois chuckled softly, shaking her head. "She's got you there, Rinaldi."

Vince shot her a look but didn't argue. Instead, he jammed his hands into his jacket pockets, a sigh escaping his lips. "It's just... all this. My shop. My parents. Alma. Marcus. It's too much. I'm barely holding it together as it is."

His candidness surprised me, and for a moment, none of us spoke. The sound of the waves crashing against the shore filled the space between us, mingling with the creak of the boardwalk beneath our feet.

"We'll figure it out, Vince," I said, my tone softening. "Whatever this is, we'll get to the bottom of it."

His blue eyes met mine, and for a fleeting moment, the frustration and fear gave way to something softer. "You sound pretty sure of yourself."

"Call it lawyerly confidence," I replied with a small smile. "But seriously, you're not in this alone. Remember that."

Lois slid her hammer back into her belt and nodded toward the shop, where officers moved in and out like ghosts. "That's right, Rinaldi. We're in this together. But right now, it looks like we're up a creek without a paddle, as they say. So I'll call it a day, if you don't mind."

I nodded. "Sounds good, Lois. I'll let you know when the sheriff clears us to work again."

Lois waved as she sauntered off, leaving just me, Vince, and Shortcake. The cat rubbed against Vince's leg, and he crouched to scratch Shorty's chin. "Guess we're not getting much work done today," he said, his tone lighter now. "Feel like taking a walk?"

I smiled, surprised by how much I liked the idea. "Sure."

Shortcake trotted ahead of us, his tail high like a proud flag. Vince chuckled. "Does he always walk like he's the king of the world?"

"Constantly," I replied, grinning. "He probably thinks he's supervising us."

We fell into step beside each other, the late-afternoon air cool and briny, carrying the occasional tang of frying oil from a seafood shack farther down the boardwalk. Gulls squabbled over scraps, their cries cutting through the rhythm of the waves.

"This whole thing's insane," I said after a moment. "A gun in the wall? Who does that?"

"I know, right?" Vince said, shaking his head. "It had to have been put there during the construction my parents did. I don't know when else it could've happened."

"You said they renovated when you were in high school?"

"Yeah," he replied, his brow furrowing. "They wanted to modernize the place. It was a big project—new walls, new floors, everything. And now that I think about it, you're right. It was around the time Alma disappeared. Which feels important."

"What do you remember about that?" I asked, watching him carefully.

He slowed, running a hand through his hair. "It was rough. Alma was... she was everything. Smart, funny, popular. The kind of person who lit up a room. When she disappeared, it was like someone sucked all the air out of the school. People were scared. And then... people moved on. Convinced themselves she ran away."

"But you didn't?"

He shook his head, his jaw tightening. "I don't think she left willingly, no. But at the time, I was a dumb kid focused on football and my girlfriend. I didn't think much about it. I regret that now."

As we reached a spot overlooking the beach, Vince leaned against the railing, staring at the horizon. Shortcake flopped onto the planks with a theatrical sigh, clearly unimpressed with the view.

"I keep thinking about that gun," Vince said, his voice low. "It has to be connected to Marcus, right? But why kill him and leave him there? Why not get rid of the body, or at least the gun?"

"It's almost like whoever did it wanted someone to find it," I said, shivering at the thought.

"Or," Vince added, "they panicked."

Before I could reply, Vince's posture stiffened slightly. His gaze shifted, locking onto a figure standing too still near the edge of a tourist shop up the boardwalk. Wyatt Parker.

Wyatt's sharp features twisted in what could only be described as disdain when he caught us looking at him. He turned abruptly and strode away, his movements stiff and deliberate.

"What was that about?" I asked him, my chest tightening.

Vince's mouth pressed into a grim line. "I don't know. But if Wyatt's hanging around, it's probably not good."

Vince's gaze lingered on Wyatt's retreating figure, his frown deepening. He stuffed his hands into his jacket pockets, his shoulders tense against the cool breeze. "It's interesting," he said after a beat. "Wyatt, wanting to buy the shop so bad. For years, I just figured it was because he wanted to build his boardwalk empire. But now I'm starting to wonder if there's some other reason he wants it so bad."

The thought sent a shiver down my spine, and I wrapped my arms around myself against the cool wind. "It's a lot of coincidence, isn't it? Wyatt wanting your shop, Marcus showing up out of nowhere, and now this gun tied to your parents' renovations?"

"Too much coincidence," Vince muttered, his voice barely audible.

We stood there for a moment longer, the rhythmic crash of the waves filling the silence. Shortcake, bored with waiting, rubbed against my legs before trotting back up the boardwalk with his tail high.

I cleared my throat, breaking the spell. "We should probably head back. It's getting colder."

Vince nodded, shoving his hands into his jacket pockets as we started walking. The fading sunlight painted the boardwalk in warm hues, but the chill in the air was unmistakable now.

As we reached the point where our paths would split, Vince turned to me, his expression softer than it had been all day. "Thanks for the walk, Ginny. I... needed that."

"Me too," I admitted, a small smile tugging at my lips. "I'll see you tomorrow? Assuming the sheriff's done with the shop."

"Yeah," he said, the corners of his mouth lifting into a lopsided grin. "We'll see if we can figure out more of this mess. And hey, if the sheriff's not done, maybe you can teach me how to bake something."

I laughed, shaking my head. "Careful, Rinaldi. You might find out you're not half-bad at it."

"Doubt it," he said with a chuckle.

With that, we parted ways, Shortcake trotting faithfully at my heels. As I made my way back to the bungalow, I couldn't shake the feeling that Wyatt's shadow loomed larger over this mystery than anyone realized.

18

Later in the day, I decided to head to the local library to dig up whatever I could about Alma. Old law school habits die hard.

The drive through Moonstone Bay felt almost peaceful—if I ignored the growing knot of anxiety in my stomach. Early February sun peeked through scattered clouds, casting a golden light on the town's winding streets and salt-sprayed store-fronts. The library was easy to find, a stately two-story brick building with ivy curling around its wooden sign.

I parked my Volvo and stepped out into the bracing sea breeze, which tugged at my jacket. Shortcake wasn't with me for this outing—I doubted he would be welcome at the library, but it hadn't stopped his protests as I'd locked him up in the bungalow.

When I stepped inside the old building, I was greeted by the unmistakable smell of a library: a mix of old paper, polished wood, and time itself. It was a scent that immediately took me back to my law school days, those long hours spent combing through case files and legal precedents in the university library.

"Good morning, hon!" a cheery voice called out, pulling me from my reverie.

Behind the counter stood a woman with short, neatly styled gray hair and a pair of glasses perched on her nose. She had the kind of welcoming smile that made you feel like you'd known her for years, even if you'd just met her.

"Hi," I said, stepping closer. "I'm new in town, and I was hoping to do a little research. And maybe get a library card, too?"

Her face lit up like I'd just said the magic words. "Well, aren't you just a ray of sunshine? I'm Barbara, and welcome to Moonstone Bay's little haven of knowledge. A library card's the perfect way to start. Let me get you set up."

She handed me a clipboard and pen, and I quickly filled out the form while she continued talking. "What kind of research are you doing? Looking for the best local hiking trails? Or maybe something more mysterious?"

I hesitated, unsure how much to share, but Barbara seemed like someone you could trust. "I'm looking into an old missing person's case," I said carefully. "The name Alma Ramirez came up recently, and I wanted to learn more about her."

Barbara's warm smile didn't falter, but her eyes grew sharper, more curious. "Ah, Alma. That poor girl. Her disappearance sure shook this town up back in the day."

"You remember it?" I asked, handing her the clipboard.

"Oh, I remember it, alright. Everyone was talking about it back then. Such a sweet girl—bright, too. Her family never did get closure." She glanced at me over her glasses. "You looking into this for a reason, or just curious?"

"A little of both," I admitted.

Barbara studied me for a moment before nodding. "Well, I'll help you however I can. The local history section's got some old newspapers and archive files. Let's see what we can find."

Barbara led me to the local history section, a cozy corner tucked away on the library's second floor. Floor-to-ceiling bookshelves lined the walls, their faded spines hinting at decades of collected town lore. In the center of the space sat an old oak table, its surface scarred with the marks of countless curious readers. A microfilm reader sat in one corner, and stacks of newspapers and archival boxes were neatly arranged on the shelf nearby.

"This here is the heart of Moonstone Bay's past," Barbara said, her voice tinged with pride. "If Alma's story is anywhere, it's in one of these."

I thanked her as she rifled through a box and then pulled a few old newspapers from the stack and placed them in front of me. "These should cover the year she disappeared. Start there, and I'll dig around to see if I can find anything else."

As Barbara moved off to rummage through the archives, I settled into a chair and flipped open the first paper. The smell of old newsprint filled my nose, and I felt a strange mix of anticipation and unease.

The headlines were a jumbled mix of small-town life: "Moonstone High Wins State Championship," "Local Restaurant Reopens with New Menu," "Fishing Contest Draws Record Turnout." But halfway down the page of one edition, a smaller headline caught my eye: "Moonstone Teen Missing After Prom."

I leaned in, my heart pounding as I read the article. Alma Ramirez, described as a bright and kind-hearted senior, had vanished the night of the prom. She'd been last seen leaving the school gymnasium with friends, but no one seemed to know what had happened after that. Search parties had scoured the area, and the town buzzed with theories, but the trail went cold.

Then my eyes snagged on a name in the article, the name of

the sheriff who investigated Alma's disappearance: Sheriff James Holloway.

The creak of the chair under me was the only sound in the room, save for the occasional soft rustle of Barbara flipping through papers across the way. I shifted, pulling the yellowed newspaper closer, the sharp tang of aged ink tickling my nose.

"Holloway," I murmured, running my finger over the byline. My pulse quickened as the name clicked into place. Sheriff James Holloway. Could he have been related to Marcus? My mind spun with the implications.

Before I could fully process it, Barbara appeared at my side, startling me so badly I nearly toppled the chair.

"Find something interesting?" she asked, holding a stack of folders that looked ready to collapse under their own weight.

I pointed to the name on the page. "The sheriff who handled Alma's case—James Holloway. Was he related to Marcus Holloway?"

Barbara leaned closer, her sharp eyes narrowing behind her glasses as she studied the name. "Now that's a connection I haven't thought about in years. Yes, James was Marcus' uncle." She straightened, her expression growing thoughtful. "James was a decent man, but he had a blind spot for his family. Didn't everyone back then?"

I nodded, her words stirring a strange mix of emotions. James Holloway. Marcus. Alma. The gun in Vince's wall. All the pieces were starting to feel like they belonged to the same puzzle—but the image was still maddeningly unclear.

Barbara set the folders on the table and gazed absently around the room. "You know, I'd nearly forgotten about that time. Marcus left town right after graduation, not long after Alma disappeared. A lot of folks thought it was just coincidence, but..." she trailed off, her gaze distant.

"But there were rumors," I prompted.

Her lips thinned. "Always, in a town this size. Some folks thought Marcus knew something about Alma. Others figured James covered something up." She shrugged, but her voice softened. "Alma's parents deserved answers, but they never got them. That poor girl..."

The weight of her words settled over me like a thick fog. The idea of Alma's parents waiting years for answers—and never getting them—made my chest ache.

Barbara placed a gentle hand on my arm, pulling me from my thoughts. "Be careful, hon. This town's got its share of skeletons, and not all of them want to be exposed."

Her words hung in the air as I nodded. "Thanks, Barbara. I'll keep that in mind."

I flipped through a few more newspapers after the librarian left, hoping for some overlooked detail that might explain how Alma's disappearance and Marcus' death were connected. But the stories thinned out as the months dragged on after her prom night. Search efforts waned, and the town moved on—or tried to.

The weight of it pressed down on me as I closed the last paper, the echo of the headlines lingering in my mind. The room felt quieter now, the rustle of old paper and the faint hum of the library the only sounds around me.

Barbara's voice startled me from my thoughts. "Any more luck, hon?" she asked, stepping back into the room with a careful smile.

"Not really," I admitted, pushing the newspapers aside. "I think I've learned what I can for now."

"Well, it's not much of a silver lining, but you've done better than most. Not many folks dig this deep into Alma's story anymore." She perched on the edge of a nearby chair, her expression curious. "So, what brought you to Moonstone Bay in the first place? Not just this mystery, I imagine."

I hesitated, brushing a speck of newsprint dust from my fingers. "I'm starting over," I said finally, surprising myself with the honesty. "I'm opening a bakery."

Barbara's face brightened. "A bakery? Oh, now that's good news! We could use one of those around here. Let me guess—cakes, bread, cookies?"

"Everything," I said with a laugh. "I've been working on the menu, but there's still a lot to figure out. Renovations, equipment, signage... It's been a process."

"Well, you've got to make cupcakes," she said with mock sternness. "I've got two grandkids who demand them on a regular basis and I'm so sick of making them I could scream," she said with a laugh. "I'd give an arm and a leg to buy some rather than baking them."

"Noted," I said, grinning. "Cupcakes will definitely make the cut."

"Good girl," Barbara said with a satisfied nod. "And you let me know when you're opening. I'll be the first one through the door—and I'll make sure the whole town knows about it."

"I appreciate that," I said, standing and gathering the newspapers into a neat stack. "Thanks for all your help today."

"Anytime," Barbara replied warmly. "And if you need a quiet place to think—or to escape the madness of opening a bakery—you know where to find me."

I paused on my way out, drawn to a display of paperbacks near the checkout desk. My eyes landed on a brightly colored mystery novel with a cheerful seaside setting on the cover. It felt fitting.

"Taking a little light reading?" Barbara asked as I handed it to her to check out.

"Something to balance out all the heavy stuff," I said.

"Smart move," she said with a wink. "Don't let those old

stories weigh you down too much, alright? You've got a bright future here—I can tell."

Her words followed me as I stepped out into the salty breeze and back to my car. The town seemed a little smaller now, its shadows a little deeper, but the flicker of curiosity in my chest hadn't dimmed.

The bakery could wait for now. Alma couldn't.

19

After leaving the library, I headed back to the grocery store to get more supplies and then back to the bungalow to try to piece together what I'd learned.

Shortcake followed me around the kitchen, meowing loudly as I put groceries away until I stooped down to give him a treat and a good long pet. Then I perched on a stool at the kitchen counter and started sifting through my grandmother's recipe book. The well-worn pages smelled faintly of vanilla and time, and the faded handwritten notes in the margins made me feel like she was right there with me. I'd been on the hunt for something comforting, a recipe that felt like home—both for myself and maybe for the bakery, if it ever got off the ground.

My mind didn't want to focus on pastries, though. Outside, I heard the wind blowing, and I wrapped my heavy sweater around myself, then thought about calling Lois to see if she could help me out with the heater. Before I reached for my phone, though, my thoughts drifted back to the threads of mystery Barbara had helped me unwind about Marcus' uncle and Alma's disappearance. Had Marcus gotten out of trouble because his uncle had been the sheriff? Had Alma's disappearance been swept under the rug to protect him?

A sharp knock at the door startled me out of my musing.
Shortcake, perched on the windowsill, flicked his tail in mild
irritation but didn't bother to investigate.

Who could it be? I didn't know many people in town. Could
Lois have read my mind and come over? Or could it be Vince?
My stomach did a little flip at the thought of Vince stopping by
unannounced. Wiping my hands on a dish towel, I crossed to
the door and opened it to reveal... Fran?

No, not Fran.

The woman standing on my doorstep looked uncannily like
Fran, but where Fran's appearance was all sharp edges and
practical functionality, this woman was a riot of flowing fabrics
and jangling jewelry. Her long, graying hair was loose and wild,
framing a face that seemed simultaneously warm and
mischievous.

"Hi there!" she said, her voice lilting and playful, nothing
like Fran's gravelly bark. She held up a lumpy piece of pottery in
a swirl of green and orange that reminded me of a tie-dye
experiment gone awry. "Welcome to the neighborhood! I'm
Faye. I live two houses over and thought I'd stop by to say hi."

"Oh! Thank you," I said, taking the pottery from her hands
gingerly. It was heavier than it looked, and its uneven shape left
me wondering if it was a vase, a bowl, or something else
entirely.

"It's a planter," she said cheerfully, reading my expression
with ease. "For herbs or succulents or whatever tickles your
fancy."

"Ah, of course," I said, still unsure whether it was meant to
be functional or decorative. "It's... unique."

Faye laughed, the sound light and musical. "Don't worry,

you'll grow to love it. Everyone does. I'm guessing by the look on your face that you've already met my acerbic twin sister?"

"Fran?"

"That's the one," she said, her bracelets jangling as she adjusted the flowing scarf draped over her shoulders. "Surprised?"

"Honestly? Yes," I admitted. "You look a lot alike, but... wow, you're really different."

She grinned, clearly relishing my confusion. "She got all the sass, and I got all the vibes. I think it worked out perfectly."

Before I could invite her in, Faye breezed past me into the bungalow, her long skirts swishing around her ankles. She took a deep inhale, turning in a slow circle as she surveyed the space.

"Well, isn't this a gem?" she said, clapping her hands together. "A little rough around the edges, sure, but I can feel the energy here—it's got potential."

She gestured toward the couch. "Mind if I sit? This is such a charming little place you've got."

"Go ahead," I said, setting the planter down on the kitchen counter.

Shortcake jumped down from his perch and sauntered over, sniffing at her long skirt. She bent down immediately, holding out a hand for him to inspect. "Oh, and who's this handsome little man?"

"That's Shortcake," I said, still clutching the planter. "He's... opinionated."

Faye grinned. "Aren't we all, darling?" She stroked Short-cake's head, and he leaned into her touch with absolute adoration.

Faye straightened, her jangly bracelets clinking together as she gestured around the room. "I've been meaning to stop by ever since Larry, down the block, mentioned someone had moved in. New blood in Moonstone Bay is always exciting. So, what brings you here? A change of scenery? A quest for self-discovery? A run from the law?"

Her teasing tone made me laugh despite myself. "Mostly the first one. But I'm opening a bakery on the boardwalk, so that's been keeping me busy. If I can ever get it off the ground."

Faye tilted her head. "Oh, Fran told me about them finding that dead man over there. How awful."

"Yeah, and this morning we found an old gun in the wall," I said, letting out a long sigh. "The sheriff shut down renovations again until he's done investigating. It's been... a lot."

Faye's brows rose, her expression turning thoughtful. "That poor man, Marcus Holloway. I remember him from back when I taught high school. He was never going to turn out well. I hate to say it." Her eyes went wide. "It sounds to me like you're caught up in something much bigger than baked goods."

I hesitated, then decided there was no harm in sharing. "I've been looking into some things from the past, trying to help Vince—he's the private investigator who owns the shop—clear his name. The sheriff seems to think he had something to do with Marcus's murder, but I doubt it."

She nodded. "Oh, I know that Vince Rinaldi. All those Rinaldi kids were so nice, so respectful. A little milquetoast for my tastes, but..." Her face grew thoughtful. "This has to do with sweet Alma, doesn't it?" Faye's voice was soft, her words more a statement than a question.

My stomach flipped. "You know about Alma?"

Faye nodded slowly. "Oh, yes. Fran and I were both teaching at the high school back when she disappeared. Alma Ramirez. She was one of those kids who just sparkled, you know? Kind, loyal, always looking out for her friends. Especially Beth Mitchell. Those two were like sisters."

"Beth?" I tried to keep my expression neutral, though my mind raced. A chill ran down my spine as I thought back to

Beth's tearful scene outside the shop on the day Marcus's body was discovered.

"Yes, Beth Mitchell," Faye repeated, her bracelets jangling as she gestured. "She and Alma had been best friends since elementary school. When Alma disappeared, it hit Beth hard. Harder than anyone else, I'd say. Took her a long time to recover."

"You were a teacher?" I asked, sitting down across from her.

"Art teacher," she said with a dramatic flourish. "I left teaching to focus on my ceramics, though. The system was stifling my creativity."

Before I could respond or ask another question, Faye changed the topic.

"You've got an interesting energy, you know," she said thoughtfully. "Grounded but restless. Focused but open to change. Have you always been this way, or is it recent?"

I blinked, unsure how to answer. "Uh... I don't know. Recent, maybe?"

She nodded knowingly, and I tried to figure out how to get back to the topic of Alma and Beth. I kept my expression neutral as my mind raced, thinking back to the crying woman I'd met in front of the shop the day we discovered Marcus Holloway's body. It was interesting that she was coming up again, and I wanted to see if Faye had any more information about her.

"Is there anything else you remember about Alma that might be helpful?"

Faye leaned back, smoothing her skirt over her knees as her eyes grew distant. "Poor Alma. I don't remember much other than what a lovely young girl she was. I don't think this town ever really recovered from losing her. And now this, all these years later... It feels like something's stirring, doesn't it?"

I hesitated, unsure how to respond. "It does feel strange, I'll admit. The timing, the connections. It's hard to ignore."

Faye nodded knowingly, then leaned forward, resting her elbows on her knees. "You know," she said, her voice dropping to a conspiratorial whisper, "if you ever want to get some real answers, I could do a séance for you."

I blinked, caught off guard. "A séance?"

"Oh, yes, darling," she said, her bracelets jangling as she gestured. "I do it all, tarot, pendulums, even a little automatic writing. Fran thinks I'm nuts, but guess who always calls me when she loses her keys?"

"That's... interesting," I said carefully, unsure how to navigate this new revelation. "But I don't think that's quite my style."

Faye waved a hand dismissively. "Oh, I get it. Lawyer brain, all logic and evidence. But let me tell you, sometimes the universe has its own way of showing us the truth. If you ever change your mind, you know where to find me."

I smiled politely, trying to imagine sitting through a séance without squirming. "I'll keep that in mind."

My phone buzzed, and I looked at the screen quickly, trying not to be rude. But as soon as I saw my ex-husband's name, I made a face and Faye laughed. I put the phone quickly down.

"Not a fan of that one, yeah?"

"My ex-husband."

She nodded knowingly. "Ah, yes. I understand perfectly. Have a few of those myself. Well," Faye said, scratching behind Shortcake's ears, "this has been delightful. But I'd better let you get back to it. I'll be just down the street if you need anything— day or night. I live in the bright pink place two doors down, can't miss it. Don't hesitate to knock."

I knew of the house. It stood out among the other soft pastel bungalows on the block like a sore thumb. "Thanks, Faye," I said, meaning it despite her eccentricities.

She stood gracefully, her myriad of bracelets jangling as she moved toward the door. "Oh, and Ginny?"

"Yes?"

Her expression turned serious for just a moment. "Be careful. Sometimes when we dig into the past, we find things that don't want to be found."

A chill ran down my spine, but I forced a smile. "I'll keep that in mind."

I walked her to the door and Faye surprised me by grabbing me and pulling me in for a hug. I wasn't a huge hugger, but I leaned in, enjoying the comfort of her embrace. "Take care. Oh, and Shortcake?" she said, craning her neck back to wave her fingers at the cat. "You come visit anytime, too. You hear?"

As the door clicked shut behind her, I glanced at the planter she'd left on the counter, its bright swirls of color both garish and endearing. Faye's warning lingered in the quiet room, an unwelcome echo of Barbara's words from earlier. Between the mystery of Alma's disappearance, the secrets tangled up with Marcus, and now the peculiar energy surrounding this little bungalow, I felt like I was being nudged toward something bigger than I'd bargained for.

Shortcake meowed, breaking the spell, and I sighed, rubbing the back of my neck. "Well, buddy," I said, glancing at the clock, "that was fun, right? Nice to be welcomed. But if I'm going to bake anything today, I better get to it."

20

After Faye left, I leaned against the counter, savoring the quiet. Shortcake was perched on the windowsill, his tail flicking lazily as he watched the seagulls flit around outside. The afternoon light slanted through the kitchen, warm and soft, but my peace was short-lived when my phone buzzed again.

I picked it up, and my stomach twisted at the sight of Christopher's name on the screen. I'd ignored his call earlier, hoping he would get the hint and leave me alone, but this time he left a voicemail. I stared at it for a long moment, debating whether to delete it without listening. But curiosity—or maybe masochism—got the better of me.

Pressing play, I braced myself as his voice, smooth and self-assured, filled the room.

"Hey, Ginny. It's Christopher." He always started that way, like I'd somehow forgotten who he was. "Listen, I've been thinking. I've got this amazing investment opportunity—huge potential, very low risk—but I need to act fast. Here's the thing: I know you've still got that beach house. It's just sitting there, right? If you sold it, you'd have the capital I need to make this work. I could offer you equity if this thing works out. We'd both benefit in the long run. Think about it, okay? Call me back."

The message ended with a sharp beep, leaving a heavy silence in its wake. My jaw clenched, and I set the phone down with more force than necessary.

"Unbelievable," I muttered, pacing the small kitchen.

Shortcake hopped down from the windowsill and sauntered over, looking up at me with a quizzical tilt of his head.

"What a piece of work," I said, rubbing my temples and glancing at the cat. "He's got a 'big idea,' Shorty. What else is new, right? And of course it's up to me to bankroll it. Give me a break."

Shortcake meowed softly, as if in agreement.

"At least this time I don't have to participate, right?" I let out a frustrated sigh, trying to shake off the lingering anger. But the more I thought about it, the more I felt it bubbling up inside me. I needed to channel it into something—anything.

Moments later, I was in the kitchen, dragging out ingredients with a fervor that bordered on manic. Flour, sugar, cocoa powder—they all hit the counter with satisfying thuds.

"Lava cakes," I announced to Shortcake, who had perched himself on a stool to observe the chaos. "Because nothing says 'I'm over it' like molten chocolate."

Shortcake meowed, pawing at the measuring spoon I'd set too close to the edge of the counter.

"No, you can't help," I said, grabbing the spoon before he could knock it onto the floor. "This is a solo mission. But you can supervise."

As I whisked together eggs and sugar, the tension started to melt away, replaced by the soothing rhythm of baking. The familiar scent of vanilla and chocolate filled the air, wrapping around me like a warm hug.

I thought back to Valentine's Day, just a few days ago, but with everything that had happened with the bakery and the dead man and the gun, it felt like a million years had gone by. Lava cakes were something I made for Christopher on our first Valentine's Day together. He hadn't been too impressed, though, and every year after that he'd always taken me out to some fancy place or other. Tonight I wanted to make the cakes for myself, enjoy the belated holiday, whether there was love in my life or not.

The batter was rich and glossy as I poured it into the ramekins, lining them up with precision. Shortcake watched from the floor, his tail flicking and green eyes locked on the bowls as if willing me to drop a spoonful.

"Not a chance, buddy," I said, sliding the tray into the oven. "Chocolate's not for cats."

The timer beeped, and I set it, stepping back to admire the tidy counter once I put everything away. My anger had dulled into something more manageable, and for the first time since Christopher had called, I felt like I could breathe.

But as I stared at the row of ramekins in the oven, a realization hit me. "What am I going to do with six lava cakes, Shorty?" I asked. He blinked at me, unimpressed. "I can't eat these all by myself."

My gaze wandered to my phone, still sitting where I'd dropped it on the couch earlier. An idea formed, and I immediately tried to shove it away. No. Absolutely not. It was reckless, and probably a terrible idea.

But the longer I stood there, the more it tugged at me. Vince had been through just as much of a whirlwind today as I had, maybe more. And I couldn't ignore how much I wanted to see him.

I grabbed my phone before I could talk myself out of it and pulled up his number.

The phone rang twice before he answered. "Hey, Ginny. What's up?"

I froze for a second, caught off guard by how warm his voice sounded. "Hey. Uh, you busy tonight?"

"Not really. Why?"

I glanced at the cakes again, suddenly feeling like this was a bigger deal than it needed to be. "I made lava cakes. Too many, actually. Thought you might want to come by and help me eat them. You know, save me from myself?"

There was a pause on the other end, just long enough to make me regret the impulsive invitation.

But then he laughed softly, the sound easing the tension in my chest. "Lava cakes, huh? Can't say no to that. What time?"

"Whenever works for you. I'm just here... baking." I winced at how awkward that sounded, but decided to let it go.

"Alright. I'll be there in a bit."

When the call ended, I stared at my phone for a moment before setting it down with a sigh.

"What am I doing, Shorty?" I muttered, turning back to the counter. The cat flicked his tail, his gaze unreadable, but I had a feeling there was judgement in those green eyes.

21

Not long after the call, a knock echoed through the bungalow. My heart did an involuntary flip. Shortcake, ever the guardian, padded to the door with his tail high, glancing back at me as if to say, *Aren't you going to get that?*

Taking a steadying breath, I opened the door to find Vince standing there, hands shoved in his jacket pockets, his hair slightly mussed from the wind. The salty evening air clung to him, mingling with the familiar hint of sandalwood.

"Hey," he said, his lopsided grin enough to make my stomach flutter.

"Hey," I replied, stepping aside to let him in. "Come on in. Watch your step, though. The place is, uh... still a work in progress."

He chuckled as he walked in, taking a quick glance around the room. "Cozy," he said with a warmth that made me feel both proud and self-conscious.

I crossed my arms, glancing at Shortcake, who was already circling Vince's legs like he was the guest of honor. "He's really taken to you," I said.

"What can I say? Cats know good company." Vince bent down to scratch behind Shortcake's ears, earning a contented purr.

The moment felt too quiet, too charged, so I blurted out the first thing that came to mind. "Sorry it's so cold in here. The heater's been acting up."

Vince straightened, raising an eyebrow. "Cold? Ginny, it's freezing. You've been living in here like this?"

"Well, yeah. I'm used to it by now," I said with a shrug. "Besides, I have blankets."

He gave me a dubious look before glancing at the old radiator in the corner. "Mind if I take a crack at it?"

"Be my guest," I said, gesturing toward it. "But I already tried everything short of kicking it."

Vince rolled up his sleeves, examining the radiator with a focused expression. "Sometimes these older units just need the right touch."

I stood to the side, arms crossed, watching as he tapped the radiator with the handle of a knife he'd grabbed from the counter. When nothing happened, he gave it a few solid whacks, and, to my utter disbelief, the heater sputtered to life with a low hum. Warm air began to drift through the room.

"Unbelievable," I muttered. "I tried that, and it didn't work!"

He shot me a teasing grin, leaning against the wall. "You don't have the magic touch. You should see me with a car engine."

I rolled my eyes but couldn't stop the small laugh that escaped. "Alright, fine. You win this round. Now, come over here and get your reward."

I moved to the counter and grabbed a ramekin, sliding a spoon into the side. The molten chocolate center oozed out just enough to reveal its gooey richness, steam rising invitingly. I topped it with a dollop of whipped cream and placed it on a plate before handing it to Vince.

"Voila, lava cake," I said, watching his reaction as he took the plate.

He eyed the dessert with appreciation. "This looks amazing."

I grabbed a second ramekin for myself, adding a dollop of whipped cream before motioning toward the small breakfast nook by the window. "Might as well enjoy it properly," I said, trying to sound casual despite the sudden flutter in my chest.

Vince followed me over, sitting across from me at the tiny table. The evening light filtering through the sheer curtains cast a soft glow across the room, making everything feel a little more intimate. Shortcake jumped onto a nearby chair, his tail twitching as he observed us like an overly curious chaperone.

"Go ahead, try it," I prompted again, picking up my spoon.

Vince took a bite, his eyes widening as the molten center hit his tongue. "Wow," he said around a mouthful. "Ginny, this is... incredible."

I smiled, feeling warmth creep up my neck. "Glad you like it."

"I don't just like it," he said, his voice softer now. "This might be the best thing I've ever tasted."

I took a bite of my own cake, savoring the rich, gooey chocolate. "It's just a recipe," I said lightly, not entirely comfortable under the weight of his gaze.

"Maybe," he replied, leaning back slightly, his eyes never leaving mine. "But it's one thing to have a recipe, and another to make something this good. You've got talent, Ginny."

The sincerity in his voice made me pause, my spoon hovering midair. "Thanks," I said quietly, not sure what else to say.

For a moment, neither of us spoke, the comfortable silence

broken only by the soft clink of spoons against porcelain and the occasional thud of Shortcake's tail against the chair.

"You know," Vince said after a while, his tone turning reflective, "this place suits you."

I raised an eyebrow. "The bungalow?"

"Not just the bungalow," he said, gesturing vaguely. "The town. The bakery. The whole thing. It's like... you're starting something here. Something good."

I met his gaze, the depth of his words hitting me harder than I expected. "That's the plan," I said softly. "It's nice to hear someone say it out loud, though."

He smiled, a little lopsided and more genuine than I'd seen all day. "Well, for what it's worth, I think you're gonna pull it off."

I studied him as we sat there, both of us quiet again. Vince was nothing like Christopher. Where Christopher had always been polished and slick, Vince was unkempt on his best days, barely holding onto life from what I could tell. But I could breathe around him. I could smile and let my hair frizz. I could wear socks with holes without getting a lecture. And I liked that. I liked it a lot.

I took another bite of cake, letting the richness melt on my tongue, but my thoughts weren't on the dessert anymore. Vince sat across from me, his expression lighter now, the weariness in his eyes softening.

"Thanks for this," he said suddenly, his voice cutting through the silence. "I didn't realize how much I needed to just... stop for a second."

I smiled, setting my spoon down. "Me neither. Sometimes it takes cake to remind you, I guess."

He chuckled, the sound low and warm. "You're not wrong." He pushed his empty plate away and leaned back slightly, his gaze meeting mine. "By the way, Donovan finished up at the shop. He cleared it, so you and Lois can get back to work tomorrow."

Relief washed over me, and a smile spread across my face. "That's great news. I was starting to worry we'd be shut down for weeks."

"Yeah," he said, his tone thoughtful. "Just... be careful, okay? Whoever put that gun in the wall, whoever killed Marcus—there's a lot we don't know yet. And I don't know if Wyatt has anything to do with what's been going on, but I don't trust that guy, not for a second."

"I will," I promised. "You, too. I know Donovan's watching you like a hawk, but don't let him get to you."

His lips quirked into a smile. "I'll try. No guarantees, though."

We lapsed into a comfortable silence, the kind that felt rare and precious, like we'd found some tiny pocket of peace amid the chaos swirling around us. But eventually, Vince pushed back his chair, standing with an easy stretch.

"I should get going," he said, his voice reluctant. "Thanks again for the cake. It was... incredible."

"Anytime," I said, rising to walk him to the door. Shortcake trotted ahead of us, his tail flicking as if to show the way.

When we reached the door, Vince hesitated, his hand resting on the doorknob. He turned slightly, his blue eyes meeting mine, and for a moment, the air between us felt charged.

"Ginny," he said softly, his voice almost hesitant.

"Yeah?" I asked, my heart pounding as I looked up at him.

Before I could process what was happening, he leaned down, his lips brushing mine. The kiss started tentative, almost cautious, but when I didn't pull away, it deepened, a slow, deliberate connection that sent warmth spiraling through me.

I leaned into him, my hand brushing against his arm, and

for a moment, the world outside the bungalow didn't exist. It was just us, standing there, caught in something neither of us had planned for, but neither of us seemed able to resist.

But then Vince pulled back, his breath uneven and his expression conflicted.

"I—" He ran a hand through his hair, stepping back toward the door. "I'm sorry, Ginny. I shouldn't have done that."

"Vince—" I started, but he shook his head, his hand already on the doorknob.

"I'll see you tomorrow," he said quickly, his tone gruff as he opened the door and stepped out into the night.

The door clicked shut, leaving me standing there, my heart racing and my lips still tingling from the kiss.

Shortcake brushed against my leg, his soft purring the only sound in the quiet room.

"What just happened?" I murmured, sinking back against the door. The cat didn't answer, but his knowing look told me he wasn't impressed with either of us.

I sighed, brushing my fingers against my lips. Whatever had just happened between Vince and me, one thing was clear—it had changed everything.

22

The next morning, sunlight streamed through the bungalow's thin curtains, waking me earlier than I'd intended. My first thought was of Vince—his lopsided smile, the way his lips had sent a jolt through me the night before. My second thought was dread. How was I going to face him today without replaying that kiss a thousand times in my head?

Shortcake, ever the helpful distraction, stretched luxuriously on the foot of the bed, his tail flicking with purpose. I sat up and scratched his back absentmindedly as I reached for my phone. Was it too early to call Lois? I bit my lip as I debated, but excitement won out. I wanted to get back to work on the bakery and I figured if it was too early she wouldn't answer.

Of course, though, Lois answered on the first ring, her voice bright despite the early hour. "Morning, demo buddy! Did you hear from the sheriff? What's the plan for today?"

I giggled and stretched. "Yep, the sheriff finished at the shop," I said, propping myself up with a couple of pillows. "We've got the all-clear to get back to work if you're up for it."

"That's what I like to hear! I'm so ready! But would you mind if Princess joins? She's been cooped up for too long, and I know she'd love to see that cat of yours again. She'll stay out of the way...probably."

I smiled, glancing at Shortcake, who gave me a sleepy, unimpressed blink. "Of course. Shorty would love to hang with his new bestie."

As I said it, my heart did a little flip. Was Lois *my* new bestie? It kind of felt that way. I hadn't had many girlfriends as an adult. Law school and my career had taken up all my energy, and Christopher had monopolized what was left. But Lois was easy to be around—funny, straightforward, and genuinely kind. I hoped this wasn't just a professional thing for her, that she wouldn't disappear on me once the bakery work was done. I hoped we'd still hang out as friends.

"Great," Lois said, her voice cutting through my thoughts. "We'll see you at the shop in about an hour. Should I bring coffee?"

"No, no," I said, as I hopped out of bed and headed for the kitchen to prep for the day. "You got it last time. Today is my turn."

"Thanks! I won't turn down free coffee! Just make mine black and strong!"

I hung up with a laugh and Shorty trailed behind me as I moved through the bungalow, his little feet padding softly against the worn floorboards. "You ready to see Princess again, huh?" I asked him, scooping kibble into his dish. "You two make quite the pair—like Lois and me, I guess. Who'd have thought we'd make friends in this little town?"

He meowed at me like he understood, then flicked his tail toward the door as if to say, "Hurry up."

I moved into the bathroom and tried to ignore my heart flip-flopping as I wondered what I should wear for the day, suddenly much more concerned now that Vince and I had shared a kiss. Would he be there today? Would things be weird between us? I hoped not, but the kiss had definitely changed things.

Throwing on a soft pink sweater and jeans, I ran some mascara over my lashes and then poured two big thermoses of coffee for Lois and I.

By the time I locked the door behind us, the cool February air nipped at my cheeks, but I felt a small thrill of excitement. Today was a fresh start—at the bakery, with Lois, and maybe even with Vince.

Shortcake shot out of the house without even waiting for me, as if he knew that something waited for him down at the boardwalk. I shook my head and sipped my hot coffee as I made the cold walk by myself.

When I arrived at the shop, the first thing I saw was Shortcake and Princess engaged in a careful sniff-off on the board-walk. Lois stood nearby, her arms crossed as she watched the two animals with amusement. Jackson leaned against the shop's exterior, fiddling with something on his phone.

"Well, look who decided to show up," Lois said with a grin as I approached.

"Hey, I'm only a little late," I said, though I wasn't sure if that was true. My nerves about seeing Vince again had made me fuss over everything from my hair to which thermos to bring, and time had gotten away from me.

"Princess has been dying to see her buddy," Lois continued, motioning toward the two animals. Princess gave a happy bark, her fluffy tail wagging furiously as Shortcake finished his inspection and padded off with a flick of his tail, clearly satisfied.

"They're fast friends," I said with a laugh, bending to scratch behind Princess' ears. The big dog turned her sweet eyes on me and gave my hand a lick, melting my heart. I could see why Shortcake liked her so much.

"Let's get inside before Jackson freezes," Lois said, nudging the shop door open.

Once we were in, the smell of sawdust greeted me. Lois and Jackson shed their jackets and got to work setting up tools, while I slid into the chair at Vince's desk, feeling a little like a trespasser.

"I found a couple of ovens that might work," I said to Lois, pulling up a website on my laptop. "What do you think about these?"

Lois leaned over, squinting at the screen. "Yeah, those are solid options. Good size, good specs. Plenty of power for a small bakery."

I exhaled in relief. "Great. I wasn't sure if I was overthinking it. I'll place the order later today."

"Perfect," Lois said, straightening. "Alright, Jackson, let's get started on that partitioned office space. You grab the saw, I'll start measuring."

As the two of them got to work, the sound of power tools buzzing in the background, I tried to focus on planning the layout for the front display. But my thoughts kept drifting back to Vince—wondering if he'd come in today, and how he'd act toward me after last night.

I didn't have to wonder for long. The door creaked open, and there he was, his blue eyes darting around the room like he was assessing the vibe before stepping fully inside.

"Morning," he said, his voice clipped.

"Morning," Lois called over the sound of Jackson hammering.

Vince nodded at her before his gaze settled on me. "Sheriff called me this morning. Said they found two sets of fingerprints on the gun from the wall."

My eyebrows shot up. "Two sets?"

He nodded, his hands shoved deep into his pockets. "They're running them now. Should know more by the end of the day."

"That's... huge," I said, exchanging a glance with Lois, who had paused her work to listen.

"Yeah," Vince said, though his tone was wary. "Could mean a lot of things. Could make things more complicated."

"Or less," Lois said, dusting off her hands as she walked over. "If one of those sets doesn't match yours, you're in the clear."

"Let's hope," Vince muttered, his jaw tight.

I leaned back against Vince's desk, crossing my arms as I stared at the half-built partition Jackson was working on. "Okay," I said slowly, letting my thoughts come together. "I'm just speculating here, but let's say Marcus did something to Alma. Like... shot her. And maybe he had an accomplice who helped him cover it up. Wyatt, perhaps? The two of them come here and hide the gun in the wall, figuring it'd get buried in the renovations. And it worked—for years. But then, for whatever reason, Marcus decides to come back for the gun. Maybe to destroy it, maybe to use it, who knows? Only this accomplice doesn't want him to. So whoever it is stops him."

Lois whistled low, leaning on the handle of her hammer. "It's not a bad theory. The timing lines up, and it explains why Marcus had a hammer with him. He wasn't here to remodel—he was here to dig."

"But why?" Vince asked, frowning. "Why would he come back for the gun after all this time? And why would the accomplice care so much about him getting it now?"

"Maybe he wanted to confess?" I suggested.

Lois shook her head. "If he was feeling guilty enough to

confess, why not just go straight to the cops? Digging out a gun wouldn't do him any good—it'd just incriminate him."

Vince crossed his arms, his brow furrowing as he stared at the floor. "Unless he thought it would incriminate someone else. Maybe Marcus wasn't coming back to confess. Maybe he was trying to get leverage."

"Leverage for what?" I asked.

Vince shrugged, looking frustrated. "No clue. And if he was using it as leverage, why would the accomplice kill him in my shop, of all places? Why not take him somewhere else?"

The room fell quiet, the weight of the questions pressing down on all of us. The only sound was the occasional clang of Jackson's tools and the faint hum of the power saw.

After a moment, I sighed, pushing off the desk. "We're going in circles. Until we know more about those fingerprints or find another clue, we're just guessing."

Lois nodded. "I hate dead ends. Feels like we're spinning our wheels."

I glanced at my phone, realizing the morning had slipped into early afternoon. "How about lunch?" I suggested, forcing some brightness into my tone. "My treat. And I'll go pick it up."

Lois smiled. "I'm not saying no to free food. Bring me back whatever sounds good."

I turned to Vince. "You too? Anything in particular you want?"

To my surprise, he shook his head. "I'll come with you."

"Oh," I said, caught off guard. "Okay, sure."

He avoided my eyes as he grabbed his jacket. "I need to get out for a bit, anyway."

Something in his tone made me wonder if it wasn't just the case on his mind. My stomach fluttered at the thought of being alone with him again, especially after last night. But I pushed it down and grabbed my own jacket, nodding toward the door.

"Back soon," I called to Lois and Jackson.

"Take your time," Lois said, already turning back to the plans on her clipboard.

Shortcake let out a disgruntled meow as I opened the door, clearly unhappy about being left behind. "You're in charge while I'm gone," I told him, scratching behind his ears.

23

Vince held the door for me as we stepped onto the boardwalk, the winter chill skimming my cheeks and snapping me fully awake. He was quiet, his shoulders drawn tight beneath his coat. My heart still fluttered from our earlier conversation—and that delicious kiss. I tried not to dwell on it, yet every time he inhaled, I remembered how close we'd been, how wonderful that kiss had felt.

We walked in silence for a few moments, the boardwalk's old timbers groaning under our footsteps. Beyond the rail, the sea was a steel-blue stretch of restless waves. A faint cry of seagulls drifted over, and the breeze carried whispers of fried dough and salt. The soft, steady sound of the tide lulled me, but under that hush, I felt the tension humming off Vince, wound too tight to ignore.

He cleared his throat. "About last night," he said, his voice careful, testing the air between us.

My stomach lurched, but I forced a wry smile. "You don't have to explain," I said, hoping to keep things light. I didn't want to show him how much I'd turned that moment over in my mind.

But Vince shook his head, stopping abruptly. I halted too, the scent of brine and wood suddenly sharper. "No, I do." His blue eyes found mine, and I could see uncertainty there. "I—I shouldn't have kissed you," he said quietly. "It was impulsive."

Impulsive. The word stung. I pressed my lips together to steady myself. "It's fine," I managed, my voice softer than I'd intended. The wind caught the ends of my hair, tossing them into my eyes. "We've both got enough on our plates. I understand."

His gaze sharpened, regret and something else flickering behind it. "I'm not good at this," he said, voice tight. "At trusting people. My marriage, the fallout—no one's ever really gotten close since. I swore I wouldn't let that happen again. But with you..."

The ocean hissed against the sand, and I could feel my pulse thrumming. "With me?" I said gently, as if afraid to startle him.

He swallowed. "It's different. I like being around you. Too much, maybe." He glanced at the sky, the horizon, anywhere but my face. "You deserve honesty. I won't pretend I can handle this easily. I like you, but I don't think I'm ready to go down that road again. I'm not ready to let myself like someone as much as I like you."

A dozen emotions tangled in my chest—warmth, uncertainty, longing. "Thanks for telling me," I said quietly. "And I don't think either of us needs an answer right now. We can just —be. For now."

The corner of his mouth lifted, an almost-smile, and something in my chest eased. We started walking again, steps falling back into sync. A gull cawed overhead. The scents of fried fish and old wood mingled, a subtle comfort in the background noise of Moonstone Bay.

Vince said after a beat, "I hope you know I'm not just cozying up to you to get out of paying that bail money."

I snorted, relieved by the hint of humor. "Oh, so that kiss wasn't a down payment? Interesting strategy, P.I."

He chuckled, the sound warm despite the cold wind. "I run a very unconventional operation. Payment plans involving smirks and hasty exits are standard."

"You mean running off and leaving me standing in my doorway? Very gallant."

Vince winced, a sheepish expression flickering across his face. "Fair. You got me there." He paused, then added with a mock-serious tone, "But I'll have you know, my running away skills are some of my best skills. It's part of my P.I. training."

"Oh, I don't know," I said, nudging him lightly with my elbow. "I've seen your desk, Vince. If disorganization is part of the curriculum, you really excel at that even more."

He laughed, the sound warm against the cool February breeze. For a moment, the tension between us from the night before melted away.

But the relief didn't last. As we neared the midpoint of the boardwalk, I noticed someone lingering by a bench, half in shadow. My heart gave a warning thump before my brain caught up: Wyatt Parker. He'd been standing there, watching us, unmoving. Now, as we approached, he straightened—a deliberate shift that felt like a dog raising its hackles.

Vince's posture changed instantly, shoulders tensing. I tasted something bitter on the back of my tongue as Wyatt stepped forward, cutting off our path. The creaking boards whined with every step. I felt my chest tighten, the distant laughter of unseen tourists suddenly stark and out of place.

"Well, isn't this cozy?" Wyatt said, voice oily, eyes gleaming. The breeze turned sharp, slicing into my cheeks as his gaze flicked between us.

"Parker," Vince said flatly. His stance went rigid. The man who'd shown me his vulnerabilities only moments ago was replaced by someone braced for a fight. The ocean murmur faded beneath the rush of my pulse.

Wyatt's smirk tilted, revealing teeth. "I thought you had more sense than to drag her into this," he said to Vince, each word clipped. "But I guess desperation makes fools of us all."

I felt Vince shift closer to me. A subtle block—my protector, my accomplice, and maybe something more. Heat flared in my chest, equal parts gratitude and anger.

"Whatever you want, say it and leave," Vince ground out. His knuckles whitened as he clenched his fists.

Wyatt's grin widened, malice lurking beneath it. "I want what's mine," he said simply, voice low. "And you know exactly what that is."

My heart hammered. I couldn't stand his smugness, the way he tried to corner Vince. The tension we'd just begun to let go of crackled back to life. I stepped forward, ignoring Vince's sharp inhale. "Why so much interest in a rundown office space?" I demanded, voice steady. "You've circled that shop like a vulture lately. Makes me wonder if you're scared of what we'll find."

Wyatt's attention snapped to me. The smirk faltered. Good. His expression darkened, eyes narrowing to slits. "You really should learn to keep quiet," he said, voice tight with anger now. "You don't know what you're getting into."

I folded my arms and tilted my chin up, refusing to budge. "Oh, I think I have a pretty good idea," I said. The breeze tugged at my coat, and behind me, Vince shifted, maybe ready to pull me back. "You and Marcus had unfinished business, didn't you? And now that he's dead...and maybe you killed him..."

"Shut up," Wyatt snarled, and in that split second, I saw something break in his control. Before I could react, he lunged and shoved me—hard.

Time stretched. For an instant, my foot caught on a gap in

the boards, and my arms flailed. Vince's hand grazed my sleeve, my name on his lips in a muffled shout. I saw Wyatt's twisted face, the boardwalk railing rushing up to meet my hip. The sound of the ocean rose to a roar in my ears as the world tilted. Just beyond Vince's shocked eyes, I glimpsed the sky and the pale winter sun, and then I was falling.

The last thing I saw before everything went cold was the terror in Vince's eyes.

24

The flashing red and blue lights cast eerie shadows over the boardwalk as I sat on the edge of the ambulance, a thick wool blanket draped around my shoulders. The paramedic crouched in front of me, her gloved hands gentle but firm as she checked my vitals.

"You're going to be alright," she said with a reassuring smile, but my thoughts were elsewhere.

Vince sat a few feet away, similarly bundled, his hair still dripping from the icy plunge. He had his head down, his elbows on his knees, and he looked utterly exhausted. I watched him for a moment, my chest tightening at the memory of his arm around me, pulling me back toward the surface.

Finally, he glanced up and caught my gaze, his blue eyes softer than I'd ever seen them. "You okay?"

I nodded, though my throat was tight. "Thanks to you."

He gave a small shrug, but his lips quirked in the hint of a smile. "Good Samaritan badge," he said lightly, though the crack in his voice betrayed him.

"Vince," I said, my voice barely above a whisper.

He looked at me then, his face drawn but open. The weight

of everything—the cold, the fear, the unspoken feelings—hung between us like the salty mist in the air.

"You saved my life," I said, the words tumbling out before I could stop them. "I—I don't even know what to say."

"You don't have to," he replied, his voice rough. He paused, then added quietly, "When I saw you go over the edge, Ginny... I don't think I've ever been so scared."

My breath caught, and for a moment, the chaos around us seemed to fade. There was something raw and unguarded in his expression, and I didn't know whether to lean into it or look away. Before I could decide, the paramedic cleared her throat.

"All good here," she said, standing and giving Vince a once-over. "You too. But you both need to stay warm and get some rest."

A bark broke through the moment, and we both turned to see Lois marching toward us, Princess leading the way and Shortcake nestled indignantly in Lois' arms.

"For crying out loud," Lois said, shaking her head as she took us in. "I leave you two alone for five minutes, and this is what happens?"

"It wasn't exactly planned," I said, my voice still shaky but steadier now.

Lois handed Shortcake to me, and he immediately began sniffing at the blanket like he was trying to figure out what had happened. "Well, you're both going back to Ginny's place. No arguments."

Vince started to protest, but Lois cut him off with a look. "Don't even try it, Rinaldi. You're both soaked, freezing, and half-dead. Come on."

Before either of us could respond, Sheriff Donovan approached, his broad shoulders cutting an imposing figure against the flashing lights. His face was set in a grim line as he glanced between us and the officers leading Wyatt Parker to a squad car in cuffs nearby.

"We're taking Parker in," Donovan said, his tone clipped. "He's under arrest for assault after what happened here today. And for the record, we were already on our way to pick him up. His fingerprints were on the gun you found in the wall. Now it's going to be a long night of questioning."

"His fingerprints?" Vince straightened, his fatigue momentarily forgotten.

Donovan nodded. "Matched them this afternoon. Didn't want to say anything until we were sure. Figured it was only a matter of time before we'd have to bring him in."

"But you don't know why they're on the gun?" I asked.

"Not yet," Donovan admitted. "That's what we're hoping to find out." He fixed Vince with a sharp look. "Congratulations, Rinaldi. You're off the hook. But don't think for a second that means I'm not watching you."

Vince rolled his eyes but didn't rise to the bait.

Donovan turned to leave, pausing only to add, "Get some rest, both of you."

As the sheriff walked away, I leaned into Lois's steady presence. "This still doesn't feel right," I said.

"No kidding," Vince muttered, scrubbing a hand through his damp hair. "Something's off."

Lois glanced between us, her sharp eyes narrowing. "Then let's figure it out tomorrow. Right now, you two need hot showers and dry clothes. Let's move."

I gave Vince a small smile as we followed Lois toward her car. Whatever else was waiting for us, at least we weren't facing it alone.

"You know, I have my own place. I could go shower there," Vince grumbled as he walked behind us.

"Nope. I want to supervise you, Rinaldi. Make sure you get

properly warm and dry. Get something other than vodka into that gut of yours."

He barely protested after that. When we got back to my place, Lois moved straight into the kitchen and started to make coffee. "You shower first, Vince, old buddy. Ginny and I need to talk. But make it quick."

Vince knew better than to argue and he grabbed the stack of Jackson's clothes that Lois had brought along and headed into the bathroom.

"Sorry for taking over," she told me as she turned the coffeepot on. "But you two looked like you could use some help."

I shivered and nodded, smiling gratefully. "We definitely could use some help," I told her.

We chatted for a few minutes as the coffee brewed and I filled her in on everything that had happened.

A few minutes later, the bathroom door opened, and Vince stepped out, Jackson's borrowed clothes hanging off him like he'd just raided a giant's wardrobe. The sleeves of the sweatshirt were rolled up haphazardly, and the sweatpants cinched tightly at the waist, yet still managed to bunch comically around his ankles.

"Looking sharp," I teased, biting back a smile.

He gave me a flat look. "I could've just gone home, you know."

"And ruin Lois's master plan to turn my place into a day spa? Never."

He shook his head, but I caught the corner of his mouth twitching. "Alright, your turn. And don't skimp on the hot water. You're still shivering."

I nodded, retreating to the bathroom with a bundle of clean clothes. I made the shower was as hot as I could bear, the steam wrapping around me like a blanket as I scrubbed the salt and cold from my skin.

But even as the water soothed me, my thoughts swirled. The icy shock of hitting the water replayed over and over in my mind, Wyatt's furious face burned into my memory. And then Vince's hand reaching out, his voice calling my name.

Why had Wyatt's fingerprints been on that gun in the wall? The pieces felt scattered, refusing to align, but one thing was clear: Wyatt had been desperate. Desperate enough to push me into the water, desperate enough to act irrationally. But was he desperate enough to kill Marcus?

I shook the thought away as I stepped out of the shower, the towel warm and soft against my skin. Dressed in sweats and a T-shirt, I felt more grounded as I padded into the living room, toweling my damp hair.

The rich, savory aroma of something cooking hit me first. I stopped short, blinking at the sight of Vince standing at the stove, a wooden spoon in one hand and a pot bubbling gently on the burner.

"You're still here," I said, a little breathless.

He turned, flashing a sheepish smile. "Figured I'd make myself useful. I found some soup ingredients in your pantry. Hope you don't mind. It's an old favorite of my ma's, 'fix anything soup' she used to call it."

"Mind?" I said, walking closer. "You're making me dinner. Why would I mind?"

He shrugged, stirring the pot. "Seemed like the least I could do after you almost drowned today. Lois had to leave."

I leaned against the counter, watching him move around the kitchen with ease.

"You're full of surprises, Vince Rinaldi."

"Don't spread it around," he said with a grin. "I've got a reputation to uphold."

The warmth in his voice and the inviting smell of soup

chased away the lingering chill in my bones. For a moment, everything felt...safe.

"You know," I said softly, "I was really scared back there. In the water."

His hand paused on the spoon, and he turned to face me, his expression serious. "Me too," he admitted. "When you went over that railing, I thought—" He broke off, running a hand through his hair. "I'm glad you're okay."

I stepped closer, my heart thudding in my chest. "Thank you. For saving me."

He hesitated, then reached out, his hand resting lightly on my arm. "Anytime."

The moment hung between us until he cleared his throat and stepped back. "Soup's ready."

We settled at the small table, bowls steaming in front of us. The soup was simple, vegetable and pasta, but it was warm and comforting, just what we both needed.

"So," Vince said after a few bites, his tone thoughtful. "Where do we go from here? Wyatt's arrested, but this doesn't feel over."

I nodded, staring into my bowl. "It's not. We don't know why Marcus was killed, and Wyatt's fingerprints on that gun just raises more questions. There's still so much we don't understand."

Vince leaned back, his gaze distant. "Do you really think Marcus came back for the gun? If so, why? And who shot him before he could get it?"

"I don't know. But I think we need to keep digging. There's more to this story, Vince. We just have to find it."

His lips curved into a faint smile, a mix of admiration and something softer. "You don't give up easily, do you?"

"Not when it matters," I said quietly.

I pushed my bowl aside, resting my elbows on the table as I looked at Vince.

"I don't think Wyatt killed Marcus," I said firmly, the words sitting heavy between us. I'd realized it in the shower, but hadn't realized why I'd thought about it until just now.

He tilted his head, his expression cautious. "Why's that?"

"Think about it," I said, leaning forward. "If Wyatt wanted to keep Marcus quiet, why would he leave his body in the one place that could lead right back to the gun in the wall?"

Vince nodded slowly, his brows knitting together. "You're right. It doesn't make sense. If he wanted to cover it up, there are a million better places to leave the body. But..." He let the word hang, clearly weighing the possibilities.

I pressed on, my voice steadier now. "But what if someone else killed Marcus? Someone who wasn't worried about the gun being found—or maybe even wanted it to be found."

His eyes flicked up to meet mine, sharp with interest. "Like who?"

"That's what we need to figure out," I said. "And I think the first step is talking to Alma's parents. They might know something—anything—that could give us more insight into what happened back then."

Vince shifted uncomfortably, rubbing the back of his neck. "That's a big ask, Ginny. They lost their daughter. Digging all that up... it could go badly."

"I know," I said, my voice softer now. "But what if it helps them too? What if we can finally give them answers after all these years? Besides, you're a private investigator. You've got every right to ask questions."

The vulnerability in his gaze caught me off guard, but he nodded after a long pause. "Okay. We'll talk to them. See if there's anything they remember that connects Alma, Marcus, or that gun."

His blue eyes sparkled as he stood and took our empty bowls to the sink.

"You saved my life today," I whispered, the words spilling out before I could stop them. I couldn't get over it.

He shook his head, a small, self-deprecating smile playing on his lips. "You're the one who keeps diving into danger. I just happened to be there to pull you out."

I stood and stepped into the kitchen, too. "I mean it, Vince. You didn't have to jump in after me, but you did. I've never had anyone do something like that for me before."

The tension in his shoulders eased slightly, but his expression remained serious. "I couldn't just let you go, Ginny."

The vulnerability in his voice cracked something open inside me. Without thinking, I wrapped my arms around him, pulling him into a hug.

For a moment, he stiffened, like he wasn't sure what to do. But then his arms came up around me, strong and steady, holding me close. His chin rested lightly on the top of my head, and I closed my eyes, letting the warmth of his embrace settle over me.

Neither of us spoke, the silence saying everything words couldn't. His grip tightened slightly, and I felt the steady thrum of his heartbeat beneath my cheek.

I tilted my head up to look at him, my heart pounding as our eyes met. The depth of his gaze, the unspoken emotions there, took my breath away. For a moment, it felt like the world had narrowed to just the two of us.

But then he stepped back, his hands lingering on my arms before he let them fall to his sides. "We've got a lot to figure out," he said, his tone lighter but his expression still serious.

I nodded, feeling the loss of his warmth but grateful for the moment we'd shared. "We do. Starting tomorrow."

His lips curved into a faint smile as he pulled away and

headed to the living area where his soggy shoes sat by the door. "I'll see you then, Ginny."

"Do you want to borrow a pair of shoes?" I asked.

He laughed. "I doubt I could even get a pair of your shoes on." He shook his head. "It's not that far home. I'll be fine."

"Goodnight, Vince," I said softly, watching as he walked to the door.

And as the door clicked shut behind him, I stood there for a moment longer, my arms still tingling with the memory of his embrace.

25

The next morning, I took my sweet time getting out of bed, savoring the rare luxury of warmth and sunlight. I felt like I might never be warm again after my dip in the ocean and it took a lot of effort to get myself out from under the covers. The space heater hummed softly in the corner at least, taking the edge off the morning chill, and golden light poured through the front window, painting everything in a soft, welcoming glow.

It was a far cry from that first morning here, when the bungalow had felt drafty and unfamiliar, and the silence had been unsettling. So much had changed in just a few short days, and yet it felt like Moonstone Bay had always been waiting for me to arrive.

I finally got dressed and padded into the kitchen with Shortcake to brew a cup of coffee and feed my cat, who seemed more subdued and less demanding this morning. I wondered how much he knew about what had happened the day before. As the rich aroma filled the air, I flipped idly through my grandmother's old recipe book, looking for something comforting to bake.

"Muffins," I murmured, landing on a recipe for blueberry muffins. "That feels like the right choice."

By the time I slid the muffin tray into the oven a little while later, the kitchen was warm with the promise of something good. I leaned against the counter, enjoying the moment and sipping my coffee, but it didn't take long for my thoughts to wander back to Marcus, Wyatt, and the gun in the wall.

"It doesn't make sense," I said aloud, glancing over at Shortcake where he sat in the front window. "Why would Wyatt leave Marcus's body in the shop, practically pointing to the gun? He had to know the police would figure it out."

Shortcake stretched luxuriously, his tail flicking as he glanced back out the window.

"Exactly," I muttered, shaking my head. "It just doesn't add up."

The ding of my phone pulled me out of my thoughts. Wiping my hands on a dish towel, I picked it up and saw Vince's name on the screen.

Morning. Just heard from Alma's mom. She's still in town and agreed to talk to us. Noon work for you?

My stomach gave a little flip—whether from the message itself or the sender, I couldn't tell.

Sounds good, I typed back. *Pick me up?*

His reply came almost immediately. *No problem.*

I glanced at the clock. That gave me plenty of time to get ready—and to figure out what exactly I hoped to learn from Alma's mom.

I went and sat out on the porch as I waited for Vince to arrive a while later. When he pulled up, I finally realized just how bad off the man was. His car looked like it had seen better decades, let alone days. The paint was dull, the passenger door handle was barely hanging on, and the muffler made an unsettling clank as I approached where he sat at the curb.

"You know," I said as I slid into the passenger seat, "they say your car reflects your personality."

Vince raised an eyebrow as he started the engine with a sputtering cough. "Good thing I'm not trying to impress anyone."

I smirked, strapping on my seatbelt. "I mean, I get it. Not everyone can afford a luxury sedan."

He shot me a sideways glance, the corner of his mouth twitching with amusement. "Yeah, well, not everyone gets a fancy law degree and the six-figure paycheck that comes with it."

I couldn't help but laugh. "I guess we'll both just have to survive with what we've got."

The banter lightened the mood as we pulled out of my driveway, but it wasn't long before the reality of where we were going settled back over us. The farther we drove, the quieter we became.

Alma's mom's house was on the edge of town and was small with a sagging front porch and a garden that had probably once been beautiful but now lay overgrown with weeds. A rusting wind chime swayed in the breeze, its soft clinks oddly mournful.

We stepped up to the door together, and Vince knocked lightly. I could hear the shuffle of feet inside before the door opened. An older woman stood there, her eyes shadowed and her face etched with lines that went deeper than age. She offered us a hesitant smile and motioned us in.

"Mrs. Ramirez, thanks for speaking to us. I'm Vince and this is Ginny," Vince began.

"Yes. Come in, come in," she said, her voice warm but tinged with weariness.

Inside, the house smelled of lavender and something faintly medicinal. Family photos lined the mantle, their edges curling with time. Mrs. Ramirez gestured toward the living room, and we sat on an old but clean couch.

She took a seat across from us, smoothing her skirt nervously. "You wanted to ask about Alma?"

Vince nodded, his voice gentle. "Yes, ma'am. We're trying to piece together some things about what happened back then. Anything you can tell us might help."

Her shoulders slumped slightly, and her hands fidgeted with the hem of her skirt. "My husband and I had a hard time with Alma. We had different values, and growing up with immigrant parents is not so easy, I know. We fought a lot. Her father especially had a hard time, God rest his soul. He didn't understand her clothes, her music, her words. It was hard for all of us."

"It broke our hearts when she chose to leave, but it was like so many other stories, you know? Teenagers are difficult. It is a difficult time, and not every family makes it through intact. I wish I would have done things differently. I wish she would give us another chance. But we never heard from her since then. I don't think I ever will."

"So you think she ran away?" I asked quietly. I hated to have to break into her reverie, but I had to know.

She nodded. "The sheriff told us that was what happened." She sniffled and looked out the window. "I thought at first maybe that boy who was always hanging around had something to do with it. But the sheriff knew that Alma left on her own."

I frowned but didn't press and wondered if the boy might have been Marcus or Wyatt and just what the sheriff had told this woman to convince her that her daughter had run away.

"It has been hard to accept, but I understand. Alma was always strong willed. She wanted to make a life for herself and it didn't include us."

Her words were heavy with grief, and I glanced around the room, searching for something to anchor myself. My gaze landed on the mantle where a row of framed photos caught the sunlight.

I stood and picked one up, studying it closely. It showed two girls with their arms slung around each other, their smiles wide and carefree.

"This is Beth, right?" I asked, holding up the picture.

Alma's mom stood and came over, peering at the photo over my shoulder. "Yes, Beth and Alma. They were best friends. Had been since they were little things. Inseparable. Beth was devastated when Alma disappeared. She kept saying that something had happened to her, that she wouldn't have run away. I wish I could have believed her."

"Beth found out she was pregnant around the time that Alma left, and I think eventually she let Alma go and focused on her baby. But it was very hard for her, almost as hard as it was for Alma's father and me."

A shiver ran through me despite the warm sunlight streaming through the windows. My mind zeroed in on Beth, on Marcus, on the gun in the wall. What did Beth know about Alma that nobody else knew? Why had she been so sure her best friend hadn't simply run away from home?

Mrs. Ramirez sat back down on the edge of her chair, her expression distant. For a moment, I thought she was done speaking, but then she glanced at the photo in my hands again.

"They used to love spending time down at Gray Pebble Cove," she said, her voice soft with memory. "It's a quiet little beach just past the boardwalk. Alma and Beth were always down there, especially in the summer. Sometimes that boy Wyatt Parker would tag along, though Alma never seemed to like him much."

My ears perked at the name, and I exchanged a glance with Vince. "Wyatt Parker?"

She nodded, her lips pressing into a thin line. "He was older, a bit rough around the edges. I never liked him hanging around the girls, but he had a charm about him, I suppose. The kind of charm that gets you into trouble."

My stomach twisted as her words sunk in. Wyatt had known Alma—and Beth. And his fingerprints were on the gun hidden in Vince's wall. The connections felt closer than ever, yet the picture remained frustratingly incomplete.

"Thank you," I said, setting the photo back on the mantle and forcing a small smile. "This has been really helpful."

Alma's mom walked us to the door, her hand lingering on the frame as she watched us step outside. "I hope you find what you're looking for," she said quietly.

"We'll do our best," Vince said, his voice firm.

The door closed softly behind us, and we walked back toward Vince's car in silence. My mind buzzed with possibilities as I replayed Alma's mom's words over and over.

"Gray Pebble Cove," I murmured.

Vince gave me a sidelong glance. "You're thinking what I'm thinking, aren't you?"

I nodded. "If Wyatt was hanging around Alma and Beth back then, there's no way it's a coincidence his fingerprints are on that gun. And if they spent so much time at that cove..." I trailed off, the unspoken thought heavy between us.

"It's worth checking out," Vince finished, his voice grim.

I glanced back at Alma's mom's house, the weight of her grief still pressing on my chest.

"We're getting closer," I said softly, more to myself than to Vince.

He nodded as he gazed out at the sky. "Yeah. But the closer we get, the messier this thing feels."

26

When we got back to Vince's car, I tried not to close the door too hard lest it fall off its hinges. The vehicle groaned in protest anyway, and I shot Vince a wary look.

"This thing has character," I teased, buckling my seatbelt.

"Yeah, well, it gets me from point A to point B... most of the time," he said, turning the key in the ignition. The engine sputtered for an alarming moment before catching.

We sat in silence for a beat, the hum of the engine filling the small space as we both processed the visit to Alma's mom.

"That was..." I started, then trailed off, searching for the right word.

"Rough," Vince finished for me, his voice low. "I can't imagine losing a child."

I shook my head and gazed out the window. The sky had turned gray, and it looked like it might rain soon. "She seems to be pretty convinced that Alma left of her own volition."

Vince frowned. "I'd bet you anything it's because that sheriff lied to her." He rubbed a hand over his face and sighed. "I guess we need to go check out Gray Pebble Cove."

I nodded, watching him out of the corner of my eye as he shifted into gear. "Yeah. Let's see if there's anything to find."

The car creaked and rattled as it rolled down the quiet streets of Moonstone Bay. The afternoon sun cast soft shadows across the pastel bungalows, and I caught glimpses of a few locals walking their dogs or tending to their flowerbeds.

As Vince steered us toward the cove, I found myself hyper-aware of how close we were in the cramped car. The scent of his cologne lingered in the air, and I couldn't help but notice the way his hands gripped the steering wheel, strong and steady.

My gaze flicked to his profile, the line of his jaw sharp and shadowed by the sunlight streaming through the windshield. There was something so... solid about him. Reliable in a way that surprised me, given how chaotic his life seemed on the surface.

The urge to reach out, to rest my hand on his thigh or lean closer, caught me off guard. I clenched my hands in my lap, resisting the impulse. This wasn't the time, and besides, I remembered his words the day before, how wary he was of a relationship, how he regretted our kiss.

Still, the thought lingered, and my heart beat a little faster as we drove in companionable silence.

When we reached Gray Pebble Cove, the car jolted slightly as Vince parked on the uneven ground. He turned off the engine, and the sudden quiet was jarring after the noise of the drive.

The cove was exactly what I'd imagined—quiet, secluded, and hauntingly serene. Small, weathered gray pebbles crunched beneath our feet as Vince and I walked along the shore, the waves rolling in with a gentle hiss before retreating back into the bay.

Shortcake would love it here, I thought absently, scanning the horizon for any sign that this place held answers.

But the longer we stayed, the less convinced I was that we'd find anything. And the more convinced I was that I'd made a big fat mistake by coming to this town, making my silly plans, and falling in love with someone who didn't want a relationship. It all crept up on me suddenly and I kicked at the pebbles, sending a spray of them into the air.

"This is ridiculous," I muttered, rubbing my arms against the chill that crept through the air. The February wind off the ocean was sharp, cutting through my jacket and stinging my cheeks.

Vince glanced over at me, his hands stuffed into his pockets. "You okay?"

I stopped walking, turning to face him. "No, not really," I admitted, the words tumbling out before I could stop them. "What are we even doing, Vince? Chasing old memories? I don't even know what I'm looking for anymore. My mom keeps calling, telling me to come back home, to give up and go back to my old life. And maybe she's right. Maybe I should've never started this."

He took a step closer, his expression softening. "Ginny, hey," he said gently, his voice steady against the crashing waves. "You can't think like that."

I shook my head, staring out at the horizon. "But what if I'm wrong? What if I'm just... stirring up old pain for no reason? Alma's mom, Wyatt, Beth—they've all been living with this for years. Who am I to dig it all back up?"

"You're someone who cares," he said simply, his voice firm. "Someone who's not afraid to ask the questions no one else will. That's not a bad thing, Ginny. It's what makes you... you."

I blinked, caught off guard by the sincerity in his tone. His blue eyes met mine, and for a moment, the world seemed to quiet around us.

"And for what it's worth," he continued, his voice softening,

"I think you're on the right track. It's messy, yeah, but the truth usually is. Don't let the mess scare you off."

The corners of my mouth twitched into a small smile despite the weight in my chest. "You're not bad at pep talks, Rinaldi."

He grinned, the tension easing slightly. "I have my moments."

We stood in silence for a bit, the wind tugging at our clothes and hair. I thought about everything we'd uncovered, everything that still didn't make sense. And then a new thought hit me.

"Lois knows Beth," I said suddenly, turning to Vince.

His brow furrowed. "Yeah, she does. Why?"

I pulled my phone from my pocket, already typing out a text to Lois. *Hey, do you think you could come with us to talk to Beth? It's about Alma. Would mean a lot.*

"I think Beth might be the key to all of this," I said as I hit send. "She was Alma's best friend. If anyone knows what really happened back then, it's her."

Vince nodded slowly, his gaze drifting back out to the water. "Let's hope she's willing to talk."

The wind picked up again, and I hugged my arms tighter around myself. But for the first time all day, I felt a spark of hope flicker in the pit of my stomach. Maybe, just maybe, we were getting closer to the answers we needed.

Vince shifted beside me, his hands shoved deep into his jacket pockets. "Hey," he said as we turned back toward the car, his voice softer now. "No matter what happens with this... I just want you to know you're doing good here. And you're one heck of a baker."

I laughed, shaking my head. "Thanks, Vince. That means a lot."

He hesitated for a moment, then stepped closer, his eyes

locking onto mine. The air between us seemed to shift, the world around us fading into the background. Before I could think too hard about it, he reached out, pulling me into a hug.

His arms were warm and solid, and I let myself sink into the embrace, resting my cheek against his chest. It felt... safe.

I tilted my head up, catching his gaze. For a moment, it felt like we were on the edge of something. His breath was warm against my cheek, his eyes flickering to my lips. Would he kiss me again? Oh, how I wished he would.

But then he pulled back, stepping away just enough to put space between us. "We should... probably head back," he said, clearing his throat.

"Yeah," I said, my voice quieter now, the moment lingering between us.

My phone buzzed in my pocket, breaking the tension. I pulled it out to see a text from Lois: *Sounds good. Come pick me up when you're ready.*

I smiled, holding up the phone. "Lois is in. Guess we'll have the whole gang together."

Vince laughed, the tension in his shoulders easing a little. "Well, that's a relief."

"You think your car can hold the three of us without falling apart?" I asked him.

He shook his head, grinning. "Don't worry. I've got more duct tape in the trunk if we need it."

We turned back toward the car, the sound of the waves behind us fading as we walked. Before climbing into the passenger seat, I cast one last look over my shoulder at the cove. The dappled sunlight danced across the rippling water, beautiful in its stillness. But there was an ache in my chest as I thought about Alma, about the secrets that had stayed buried here for so long.

"We'll figure it out," Vince said, as if reading my thoughts.

I nodded, slipping into the car beside him. As we pulled away from the beach, the cove disappeared from view, but the weight of its mystery stayed with me.

27

Vince's car wheezed to a halt outside Lois's workshop a few minutes later, and I winced as it let out a loud clunk, followed by a hiss that didn't sound reassuring. I glanced at Vince, but he just grumbled something under his breath and slammed the gearshift into park.

Lois appeared in the doorway, a shop rag slung over one shoulder. "You know," she said, climbing into the back seat with a grin, "I've seen more stable carnival rides than this thing."

"Yeah, well, you could always walk to Beth's house," Vince shot back as he adjusted the rearview mirror.

Lois smirked, unfazed. "Relax, Rinaldi. I'm just joshin',"

I glanced over at him as she buckled in, but his jaw was set, his focus glued to the road, and I couldn't tell what he was thinking. The car rattled as we drove through town, the engine sounding like it might give out at any second.

We drove in silence for a bit before Lois spoke up. "So, what's the plan here? Beth's not exactly known for being chatty."

"I'm thinking we just ask her about Marcus again," I said,

turning back to look at Lois. "See if she remembers anything else about that night. Maybe she knows something she didn't think was important at the time."

"And what if she doesn't want to talk?" Lois asked, raising an eyebrow.

"Then we thank her and leave," Vince said. "This isn't an ambush."

Lois nodded and sank back into the seat as she gazed out the window.

Beth's trailer park came into view as we rounded a bend. It was tucked away on the edge of town not far from where Alma's mom lived. It was the sort of place where time seemed to stand still. Faded siding and sagging porches lined the narrow gravel road, and a few kids played in the yard of one of the better-kept homes.

Beth's trailer was at the far end, almost hidden behind a line of overgrown shrubs. A child's tricycle leaned against the porch, its bright red paint chipping away.

Vince's car groaned to a stop on the uneven gravel driveway in front of Beth's trailer. I stepped out onto the loose gravel, shivering as a sharp gust of wind sliced through my jacket. The trailer stood at the edge of the lot, its aluminum siding battered from years of salt-laden air. A frayed curtain hung crooked in the front window, and I saw it move as the three of us made our way up the drive.

Vince walked ahead of us, his boots crunching on the gravel. "Let's make this quick," he muttered, his shoulders rigid.

As we approached, a dog barked in the distance, followed by the faint slam of a screen door from one of the neighboring trailers. Vince knocked, the sound echoing hollowly against the flimsy metal frame.

Beth opened the door after a long pause, her face pale and lined with exhaustion. She glanced between the three of us, her brows knitting together in suspicion, and she glanced at Lois. "Didn't expect such a crowd," she said, her voice tight.

"We're sorry to bother you," I began, stepping slightly forward. "We just wanted to ask a few questions about Marcus."

Beth hesitated, her fingers gripping the edge of the door so hard her knuckles turned white. For a moment, I thought she might slam it shut, but then she sighed and stepped back, motioning us inside.

The trailer's warmth was stifling, thick with the smell of reheated coffee. Toys were scattered across the floor—a mismatched plastic truck, a few action figures missing limbs. A frayed blanket hung over the back of a recliner that looked as if it might collapse at any moment.

Beth motioned toward the couch, and I sat down while Lois took the armchair. Vince stayed near the door, leaning against the wall with his arms crossed, his gaze sharp and watchful.

"So," Beth said as she sank into the recliner, her movements stiff and slow, "what do you want to know?"

I hesitated, searching for the right approach. "I was wondering if there was anything else you remembered about the night Marcus came to see you. The night he died."

Beth's lips thinned, and she avoided my gaze, staring instead at the cluttered coffee table between us. "I told the sheriff everything," she said flatly. "He showed up, we talked, he left. That's it."

Her voice lacked conviction, and my pulse quickened as my mind suddenly clicked on something. "What about the hammer?" I pressed gently. "Did he get it from you?"

Beth's head snapped up, her eyes narrowing. "The hammer?" she repeated, her voice rising slightly. "No. He didn't get it from here. He must've had it with him when he came to Moonstone Bay."

The certainty in her tone sent a chill down my spine. My mind raced as I connected the dots—Beth shouldn't have known about the hammer that Marcus had had unless someone had told her...or unless she'd seen it herself. And other than Vince, Lois, and I, the only other person who would have told her was the sheriff, and I doubted he would have let that crucial piece of evidence slip.

I exchanged a glance with Vince, who gave me a barely perceptible nod. Lois sat back in the armchair, her arms crossed as she studied Beth with a steady, unreadable gaze.

I cleared my throat, deciding to try another angle. "What did Marcus think about your son?"

Beth's posture stiffened, and her hands curled into fists on her lap. "He barely even cared about Alex," she said bitterly, her voice trembling with suppressed anger. "He said he couldn't do anything about it. Can you believe that? After all these years! To find out you have a child and just brush it off like a speck of dust on your coat?"

Her anger filled the cramped space like smoke.

I took a steadying breath, the pieces of the puzzle clicking into place. I wasn't certain it was the right thing to do, but I couldn't have stopped myself if I'd tried. "Is that why you killed him?" I asked quietly.

Beth's head snapped up, and for a moment, it was like staring into a storm. Her eyes flashed with anger and grief, her voice trembling as she spat, "You don't know what it's like. Living with this... this secret. It eats at you, bit by bit, until there's nothing left."

I swallowed hard, keeping my voice steady. "What secret, Beth? Help us understand."

She was silent a long moment, and I wondered if she would answer. But then she looked straight at me. "I saw them," she said, her voice breaking. "All those years ago. I saw Marcus and Wyatt that night. The night Alma disappeared."

My stomach dropped, and Lois sucked in a sharp breath. Vince tensed beside me, his gaze locked on Beth.

"They were drinking down by Gray Pebble Cove," Beth continued, her voice shaking. "I don't know what started it— maybe she said something they didn't like, maybe they were just being cruel—but it got ugly. They... they killed her. Right there on the beach. They shot her." Her voice cracked, and she pressed a hand to her mouth, tears spilling down her cheeks.

I felt my heart hammering in my chest, the weight of her words sinking in like a stone.

"Why didn't you go to the police?"

Her voice rose, raw with emotion. "I was eighteen! And Marcus was his nephew. I knew he would've swept it all under the rug, just like he did everything else. So I stayed quiet. I told myself it wasn't my fault, that I couldn't have stopped them. But that didn't make it any easier. Not a single day has gone by that I haven't thought about Alma. About what they did to her."

Beth sank into the recliner, her body shaking as she wept. Vince stepped forward, but she held up a hand, stopping him in his tracks.

"When Marcus came back," she said, her voice thick with grief and rage, "it was like ripping open an old wound. He had the nerve to come here, to brush off my son, to act like he was better than me. Like he didn't have blood on his hands. I couldn't... I *couldn't* let him get away with it any longer."

Her voice turned hollow, her gaze distant. "I knew he was going to the shop. I knew he wanted the gun because he talked about getting something from Wyatt and the only way that would have happened was if he blackmailed him. I saw back then where they put it and as soon as he grabbed the hammer from my shed, I knew what he was up to. He wasn't coming back to make amends or come clean—he was coming back to blackmail Wyatt. So I followed him. I thought... I thought if I killed him there in the shop, if I left the body, the police would have to dig deeper. They'd have to find the gun in the wall. They'd have to find the truth. And I could stay out of it."

I felt a shiver run down my spine, the pieces falling into place. "So you shot him," I said quietly.

Beth nodded, her hands trembling. She stood up and started to pace, her whole body radiating with energy. "I followed him to the shop and watched as he busted the window, waited until he was distracted, then... then climbed in and pulled the trigger. And then I ran. I thought it would be enough. I thought it would all come out. But now..." Her voice broke, and she buried her face in her hands.

The room fell silent, the weight of her confession pressing down on all of us.

Vince took a cautious step forward, his voice calm and steady. "Beth, I know you were trying to do the right thing. But this... isn't right. We're going to have to tell the sheriff."

Beth's head snapped up, her eyes wide with panic. Her hand darted to the side table, and before I could react, she pulled out a small revolver, her hands shaking as she pointed it at herself.

"Beth, no!" I cried, my heart pounding in my chest.

"You don't understand," she said, her voice breaking. "I've ruined everything. My son—what's he going to think if I go to jail?"

"It won't be as bad as what he would think if you took your own life," Vince said, taking a cautious step closer. "Think about what that would do to him, what he would carry for the rest of his life. He's already lost so much—don't take his mother away too."

Tears streamed down her face, her grip on the gun faltering.

"I just wanted the truth to come out. I wanted to make him pay. I miss her so much," she whispered.

"And it will," I said softly, my voice trembling. "The truth will come out. But you need to be here for your son now. And you need to tell your story, Beth. Alma deserves that. Your son deserves that."

For a moment, the only sound in the room was Beth's ragged breathing. Then, slowly, she lowered the gun, her shoulders sagging as if the weight of the world had finally crushed her.

Vince stepped forward and gently took the weapon from her hands, setting it on the coffee table.

I let out a shaky breath, my hands trembling as I pulled out my phone. "I'll call the sheriff," I said, my voice barely above a whisper.

28

Three weeks later, the memory of that day at Beth's trailer still clung to me like a shadow. It was strange how life could twist so sharply in such a short time. One moment, you were begging someone to put down a gun; the next, you were designing cupcake menus and ordering espresso machines.

The morning sunlight streamed through the bungalow's window, warming the soft throw I'd cocooned myself in. I'd spent most of the previous night baking like a madwoman to get ready for the bakery's grand opening and I wasn't ready to get out of bed quite yet. But Shortcake was perched like a tiny emperor on my stomach, his green eyes drilling into me. He let out a commanding meow, urging me to rise.

"Alright, Your Majesty," I said, scratching behind his ears. "I'm getting up. Big day today."

The words felt surreal as they left my mouth. Not too long ago, I was living an entirely different life. Opening the shop would propel me into a completely new existence. But I was more ready than ever.

I swung my legs off the bed, feeling a shiver of excitement

rather than cold. The bungalow was still a work in progress, but it felt more like home with every day that passed. The heater hummed softly in the corner—a small miracle courtesy of Vince —and I smiled as I thought back to how far I'd come since that freezing first morning here in Moonstone Bay.

Just as I was about to start my day, my phone buzzed on the nightstand. My mom's name lit up the screen. I hesitated before picking it up, memories of our last conversation prickling at the edges of my mind.

"Hi, Mom."

"Virginia," she said in her trademark crisp tone. "I'm getting ready to leave here soon. I'll be there in an hour or so."

My heart skipped a beat. "Wait, you're coming today?"

"Of course. You think I'd miss the grand opening of my daughter's... bakery?" Her tone softened slightly on the last word, as though she were trying it out. "I still don't understand why you left a perfectly good law career, but... I want to see it for myself."

I'd finally broken the news of the bakery to her about a week before. She hadn't taken it very well at first, but she'd been more supportive than I'd expected.

I pressed my lips together to keep from snapping back. Progress was progress. "Thanks, Mom. That means a lot."

There was a pause on the other end before she said, "Do you need anything? I could stop and pick up flowers or—"

"No, it's all set. Just bring yourself."

I said goodbye and hung up, then flopped back onto the bed with a groan. Shortcake hopped up, clearly displeased by the interruption, and I gave him a rueful smile. "Think we can get through today without making a scene?"

He blinked at me and I laughed.

I wasn't planning on letting him into the shop for the most

part, but I figured he could act as mascot on opening day, at least.

I sighed and pushed myself off the bed, the nerves fluttering in my stomach intensifying with every step. After a quick shower, I tugged on my favorite sweater and jeans—comfortable but polished enough to look presentable. Shortcake trailed behind me as I moved through the bungalow, pacing between packing a tote bag and triple-checking my to-do list.

"Signs, check. Menus, check. Money, check," I muttered under my breath, trying to ignore the way my hands shook. "Everything's fine. It's going to be fine."

Shortcake meowed at me, brushing against my legs, and I crouched down to give him a quick scratch behind the ears. "Thanks for the pep talk, buddy."

He purred, his judgment seemingly suspended for now, and I scooped up my bag, slinging it over my shoulder.

As we walked down the quiet street toward the bakery, the crisp morning air sent a pleasant shiver down my spine. The sky was an endless blue, dotted with a few wispy clouds, and the scent of salt and seaweed wafted in on the breeze. A few seagulls called to each other, their cries echoing off the colorful facades of the shops lining the boardwalk.

The bakery came into view as I hit the planks of the boardwalk, its freshly painted sign gleaming in the sunlight. My chest swelled with pride at the sight of it. The past week had been a blur of activity: unpacking mixers and ovens, testing recipes until the kitchen smelled permanently like sugar and butter, and watching Lois transform the space from a dusty, neglected office into a warm, inviting shop.

Lois wore her trademark overalls, hands on her hips as she squinted at the newly painted window. Vince, leaning casually against a pillar, shot me a crooked grin as I approached. Shortcake trotted ahead of me, his tail swishing like a metronome.

"Well, there she is," Lois said, grinning. "Finally decided to join us."

"Had to make sure I looked good for opening day," I said, adjusting my sweater.

Vince grinned. "You look great. It's the sign we were debating. You sure about this?"

I followed his gaze to the gleaming new sign in the window. The words *Moonstone Bakery* were painted in a big, soft, cheerful script. Below it, in smaller, elegant lettering, was *Rinaldi Investigations*.

Lois tilted her head. "It's... unique. I'll give you that."

"It's perfect," I said, feeling the warmth of pride bloom in my chest. "A little strange, sure, but it's ours."

Vince chuckled. "Strange might be an understatement, but hey, it fits this town."

A small group of early risers had gathered a few paces away, their curiosity evident as they chatted and glanced at the shop. My nerves buzzed, but I swallowed the lump in my throat.

Before I could step forward, a familiar voice cut through the crowd behind me. "Virginia?"

I turned, my breath catching as I spotted my mother. She was dressed impeccably, as always, in tailored slacks and a crisp white blouse, her leather bag slung over one shoulder. Her sharp eyes took in the bakery sign, and her mouth pressed into a thin line.

"Well," she said, her tone carefully neutral as she took in the sign. "You didn't mention the investigating part of your new venture."

Heat rose to my cheeks, but before I could respond, Vince stepped in, extending a hand with an easy smile. "You must be Ginny's mom. Vince Rinaldi. Private investigator—and proud cohabitant of that sign."

Lois followed suit, her grin as wide as ever. "And I'm Lois

Wheeler. Construction magician, cupcake enthusiast, and general chaos wrangler. Good friend of Ginny's. It's a pleasure."

My heart swelled as she said the part about being my good friend, and I grinned at her.

My mom's eyes flicked between them, then landed back on me. "Interesting friends you've made here."

"They grow on you," I said, shooting a pointed look at Vince and Lois, who both smirked unapologetically.

"Well," my mom said again, eyeing the crowd now gathering near the bakery door. "I'll say this much—it's charming. And busy, by the looks of it."

"That's the hope," I said, the tension in my chest easing slightly. "Thanks for coming, Mom. It means a lot."

Her expression softened for a moment, a rare flicker of approval crossing her features. "I wouldn't miss it."

Lois nudged me again, breaking the moment. "You gonna say something, boss?"

I stepped forward, the moment suddenly feeling monumental. The past few weeks flashed in my mind—Beth's tearful confession, the endless hours of work to get the shop ready, and the growing bond between the three of us that had somehow turned Moonstone Bay into home.

I turned to Vince and Lois, and then to the small crowd. "Thank you all for being here today," I said, my voice steady despite the fluttering in my chest. "Opening this bakery is a dream I didn't even know I had until I came here. And now that it's real, I'm just... so grateful to all of you for helping me make it happen."

The crowd clapped politely, and Lois gave a low whistle. Vince's grin widened, his blue eyes sparkling.

"Alright," I said, turning back to the door. The sign hung in my hand, its cheerful *Open* side gleaming in the sunlight. With one last deep breath, I hooked it onto the door and flipped it over.

The little bell above the door jingled, and I stepped aside with a broad smile. "Come on in!"

The crowd surged forward, Shortcake weaving expertly through the commotion like the self-appointed mayor of the boardwalk. Lois shot me a thumbs-up, and Vince gave me a look that said, *You've got this.*

And for the first time, I truly believed I did.

———

You've come to the end of Lava Cake and Lies! But did you notice how Vince called Shortcake "Chicken Wing" in the beginning of the story? Want to know why?

Sign up for my newsletter and get an exclusive bonus story absolutely FREE! - Just follow the link (or visit my website at novawalsh.com) to sign up! http://bit.ly/3BtAQFW

This very special bonus scene was the first spark of inspiration for the Moonstone Bakery series, and even though it didn't make it into the book, I'm thrilled to share it with you!

I promise to keep your inbox cozy, not cluttered! You'll receive the occasional release and sale information only when you sign up!

———

Want to know what happens next with Ginny, Vince, Lois, and Shortcake? Book two in the Moonstone Bakery series, Cupcakes and Crime, is available for preorder now!

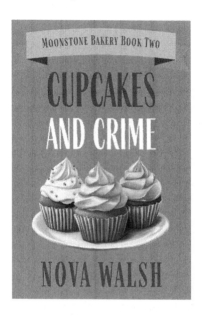

The ovens are warm, the cupcakes are frosted, and Ginny Malone is about to bite off more than she can chew...

Ginny and her mischievous cat Shortcake are finally settling into life in Moonstone Bay. Her coastal bungalow might still need a little TLC, but her bakery is open, her friend Lois is never far away, and she's even landed a big cupcake order to boost business. Everything seems to be falling into place—until her charmingly grumpy landlord, private investigator Vince Rinaldi, takes on a client whose problems lead straight to murder.

With Vince pulled into a tangled web of lies and secrets, Ginny can't resist lending a hand—or her legal expertise. But balancing bakery orders with sleuthing isn't easy, especially with renovations going sideways, quirky locals causing a stir, and a killer who might be closer than anyone suspects.

As Ginny, Lois, and Vince dig deeper, they'll need to rely on teamwork—and maybe just a little luck—to solve the case before someone else gets hurt.

Cupcakes and Crime is a heartwarming and suspenseful cozy mystery filled with endearing characters, a dash of romance, and recipes you'll want to try.

Preorder Cupcakes and Crime today and treat yourself to the next delicious mystery in the Moonstone Bay series!

GINNY'S LAVA CAKE

Oozy gooey chocolate is great for any situation! Make sure to eat these warm from the oven to get the full deliciousness.

Ingredients:
- 1/2 cup unsalted butter
- 4 ounces bittersweet chocolate, chopped
- 1 cup powdered sugar
- 2 whole eggs
- 2 egg yolks
- 6 tablespoons all-purpose flour
- 1 teaspoon vanilla extract
- A pinch of salt

Instructions:

Preheat your oven to 425°F (220°C). Grease four ramekins and place them on a baking sheet.

In a microwave-safe bowl, melt the butter and chopped chocolate together in 30-second intervals, stirring each time until smooth.

Stir in the powdered sugar until well combined. Add the eggs and yolks, whisking until the batter is smooth and glossy.

Stir in the vanilla extract and salt.

Gently fold in the flour until just incorporated.

Divide the batter evenly among the prepared ramekins.

Bake for 12-14 minutes, until the edges are set but the centers are still soft.

Let the cakes cool for 1 minute, then carefully invert each onto a plate.

Serve immediately, optionally with a dusting of powdered sugar or a scoop of vanilla ice cream.

VINCE'S FIX ANYTHING SOUP

The soup that warms hearts, fixes bad days, and uses whatever you've got!

This is a no-stress, no-rules recipe inspired by Vince's mom. It's perfect for when you want something cozy but don't have time for a grocery run. The beauty of "Fix Anything Soup" is that it's adaptable—just like Ginny is learning to be.

Ingredients:
- 2 tbsp olive oil (or butter, if that's what you've got)
- 1/2 medium onion, diced
- 2 cloves garlic, minced
- 2-3 cups assorted veggies (carrots, celery, zucchini, spinach, or whatever's in the fridge)
- 6 cups chicken or vegetable stock
- 1 can of diced tomatoes (14.5 oz)
- 1-2 cups uncooked pasta (any shape—elbows, shells, or broken spaghetti work wonderfully)
- 1 tsp dried Italian herbs (basil, oregano, thyme, etc)
- Salt and pepper, to taste

- Optional: shredded chicken, cooked sausage, or beans (for extra heartiness)
- Fresh parsley or Parmesan cheese, for garnish

Instructions:

Heat the olive oil in a large pot over medium heat. Add the diced onion and garlic, and sauté until fragrant and golden. This is the soul of the soup—don't rush it!

Toss in whatever vegetables you have, aiming for about 3 cups total. Carrots and celery are classic, but don't be afraid to add chopped zucchini, kale, or even frozen peas. Sauté for 3-4 minutes to soften them up.

Add the chicken or vegetable stock, scraping up any browned bits from the bottom of the pot. Stir in the can of diced tomatoes, including the juice.

Sprinkle in the dried Italian herbs, a pinch of salt, and a good crank of black pepper. Bring the soup to a boil, then reduce to a simmer. Let it bubble gently for 10-15 minutes to let the flavors meld.

Stir in the pasta and cook until tender, about 8-10 minutes, depending on the shape. If you're adding protein like shredded chicken or sausage, now's the time to toss it in, too.

Give it a taste and adjust the seasoning. Need more salt? Pepper? A dash of hot sauce? Let your taste buds guide you.

Vince's Pro Tip:

"Don't overthink it. If you've got a can of beans instead of tomatoes, or rice instead of pasta, throw that in instead. The only wrong way to make this soup is to forget the love."

Enjoy this simple, hearty soup that's perfect for fixing just about anything—even a bad day!

ALSO BY NOVA WALSH

THE SUGAR CREEK MYSTERY SERIES

Love cozy mysteries with a side of delicious treats? Check out my Sugar Creek Mystery Series, where small-town sleuths solve crimes and whip up culinary delights!

Death and Wedding Cake

Death and Peaches

Death and Fondue

Death and Blackberry Pie

Death and Eggnog

Death and Groom's Cake (Coming February 2025)

Christmas in Sugar Creek (Short Story Collection)

THE MOONSTONE BAKERY MYSTERY SERIES

Lava Cake and Lies

Cupcakes and Crime (Coming March 2025)

THE MAPLE GROVE ROMANCE SERIES

The Cozy Corner Book Store

The Sugar Stop Chocolate Shop

ABOUT NOVA WALSH

 Author Nova Walsh writes culinary cozy mysteries full of humor, shenanigans, and friendships that last a lifetime. She mixes in a healthy dose of amateur sleuthing, some slow-burn romance, and a pinch of comedy in every book she writes.

Nova is a former chef/caterer who still loves to cook but loves to write even more. She's an enthusiastic, if not totally successful gardener and loves travel, wine, and hanging out with friends.

Nova lives in central Texas with her husband, son, and two delightfully crazy pups. When she isn't writing, she's often cooking, gardening, hiking, or reading a good book with a pup by her side.

You can contact Nova at nova@novawalsh.com

Made in the USA
Columbia, SC
09 March 2025

54895695R00121